BI

Originally published on AMAZON

This re-edited edition publish........................

Front Cover art by Paul Draper

Contents:

I see your candle is burning bright.

Splendid.

Just as well considering the power cut.

Are your neighbours lights out too; or is it just your house?

Don't bother to check.

I know it's just you ...

and me.

1.

The black twisted roots of this taphophile tale are planted in the soil of my paternal family tree. Several of my Victorian and Edwardian ancestors are buried in the cemetery where the ghostly goings on take place. St. James' Cemetery (originally a stone quarry in operation from the 16th century to 1825) is Liverpool's largest burial ground; between 1829 and 1936, 57,774 people were laid to rest within its walls. My tale takes place there a few years before the controversial decision was made to clear away most of the headstones and turn it into a Public Garden.

THE GHOSTS OF ST. JAMES' CEMETERY

by Marc Damian Lawler

Location: St. James' Cemetery; fifty feet below street level. Liverpool Anglican Cathedral towering above.

(June 24th, 1964)

GRAVE DRAWINGS

Penny Newton put down *The 5th Pan Book of Horror Stories* and glanced at her watch which was pinned upside down on the breast of her green-striped uniform. Ten to two; plenty of time before resuming her split shift at the Homeopathic Hospital on Hope Street.

She always sat on the same bench - the one nearest to the subterranean stone tunnel (she always experienced a pleasurable shiver when walking through its gloomy interior) - digesting a spooky story or two and her sandwiches.

Her mind wandered back to the story she'd just finished reading: *The Confession of Charles Linkworth* by E. F. Benson. A line towards the end - "'Something is coming!' said the doctor' - con-

3

tinued to effect her. Her late father had been a doctor, and she'd imagined it was him saying the line to her from beyond the grave.

She read the line again, and this time heard him say *someone* instead of *something* is coming!

A worry worm wriggled about in her head.

No one else was in the cemetery; or at least, no one in plain sight. There were plenty of trees and bushes to use as cover.

Usually there were others down there; a bunch of art students smoking and drinking and doing very little art work; or an elderly couple tottering along the path that wound its way around the hundreds of headstones.

She was about to get up and go when her attention was drawn to a girl - whom she was certain had not been there a second ago - pushing a pram on the path towards her.

Right away she knew that the girl was a ghost. Not because she could see through her; or any other obvious reason like that, but because - to her amazement - she could hear her thoughts, as well the words she spoke out loud.

Her speaking voice was exactly in keeping with the age she looked; but her thinking voice was that of a croaky old woman's.

"How long have we been wheeling this coffin around this pit of bones?"

"Forty one thousand, six hundred and ten days," she answered in her age appropriate voice.

"Dear God! Burning to death was a breeze compared to this perpetual boredom."

"You shouldn't say such evil things."

"Shut your mouth and keep pushing."

Penny was trying to work out what she was going to say or do when the girl drew level with the bench, when a man wearing an oil paint encrusted artist's smock appeared out of nowhere directly in front of the bench. She could see he was a ghost too, because the right side of his face - just like the face on the cover of the book she was reading - was an empty eye-socket skull. In his liver-spotted hands he held a frayed at the edges sketchbook and a gold cased pencil.

He began to draw her. His left hand making rapid, confident marks on the page; and despite his dreadful appearance, she felt flattered by the attention and brushed her wavy black hair away from her heart-shaped face.

"What beautiful green eyes you have."

"Thank you," she replied.

He opened his mouth in surprise and his pipe fell out. "Oh, dear Lord! Can you hear me?"

"Yes - and see you."

"I'm terribly sorry, my dear. I must be frightening you out of your wits!"

"Do I look frightened?"

"As a matter of fact, you don't. That's strange. Most people panic when they see my face for the first time." He leaned down and picked up the pipe. "Do I look as bad as everyone says I do?"

"Who's everyone?"

"The other ghosts."

"Here in the cemetery?"

"Yes."

"How many are there?"

"Hard to put an exact number on it... but of the regular ones, I'd say about four hundred."

"Four hundred?!"

"Considering that more than fifty thousand people are buried here, that's an exceptionally low number. Of course, that number increases significantly on special occasions. Such as in 1904, when Edward VII attended the laying of the Cathedral's foundation stone. That day, ten thousand or more materialised!"

"Were you one of them?"

"Yes, but not by choice. I've been haunting this place since the autumn of 1880." He sighed theatrically, and the ghost of a flesh-eating beetle scurried out of his mouth and wasted no time going back in through his empty eye socket.

He started to sketch her again.

"Were you a professional artist?"

"I was indeed."

"What was your name?"

"My name *was* and still *is* William Daniels."

"Sorry. I didn't mean to refer to you in the past tense."

His half frown smoothed out. "Apology accepted, my dear."

"I think I've seen one of your paintings in the Walker Art Gallery."

"I should hope so! After all, I was known as the Rembrandt of Liverpool."

As the ghost girl drew level with the bench, Penny was surprised to hear someone speak from within the perambulator.

"Who's Mr. Daniels sketching?"

"The nurse from last week."

"Bring me along side, I want to see."

"Yes, Miss Biffen."

Penny wanted to peek inside the pram, but thought it would be rude to move out of the artist's right eyeline.

"Pull the hood down, I want to see properly."

Again, the ghost girl did as she was told. But, inwardly, granny-grumbled about it.

Penny found it hard not to stare when she saw who the voice belonged to - a chubby-faced, middle-aged woman with no arms, and what must have been very short legs.

"Far be it from me to cast a critical eye..." said Biffen to Daniels, "- but are you quite sure that's the correct shape of her mouth?"

"Considering I have only one eye to study her with, I believe I've captured her likeness admirably well."

"That's just an excuse not to get it right. I was born with no arms, but that didn't stop me from having my paintings on display at The Royal Academy and..." She sat up as straight as she could, "from painting the Royal Family!"

"Only because they felt sorry for you."

"That is a lie!"

He stared at her with his one piercing eye. "It's the truth, and you know it."

"I know no such thing!"

"Your whole artistic career was built around your disability. For heaven's sake, woman - people paid to watch you paint with your mouth!"

"That was only part of it."

"No, that was all of it. You *were*, and still *are*, a curiosity, nothing more."

"Tell me, sir... How many members of the House of Hanover sat for you in your lifetime?"

7

"For your information, madame... I turned down a royal commission; and the opportunity to paint the Duke of Wellington. But I'll tell you who I did paint; although sadly not from life - Napolean Bonaparte!"

"Why you Republican rascal. If I were a man, I'd knock you down!"

He pushed the pram away as he puffed on his pipe and chuckled.

Miss Biffen protested loudly, and the ghost girl wheeled her back.

As the argument raged on, Penny decided it was for the best if she quietly slipped away. She decided to return to street level via the archway at the south end of the cemetery.

"No, don't go that way!" warned the ghost girl.

"Why not?"

"Someone bad is there."

Penny cast her eyes in that direction... but couldn't see the area itself because the path curved around a corner.

"Is it a bad ghost?"

"No - a bad man - a murderer."

Mr. Daniels broke off the argument to ask: "My dear, to whom are you talking to?"

"The girl."

"What girl?"

"That girl."

His eye followed her finger to where she was pointing, but his half expression drew a blank.

"He can't see her," said Miss Biffen. "Never has, and probably never will."

"Who does he think pushes the pram?"

"Who knows? Probably the wind."

"The pram is bewitched," answered Mr. Daniels.

Louisa laughed sweetly, but her inner-voice huffed.

Biffen asked Daniels to wheel her there; so she could get a good look at the murderer.

"What about your invisible attendant?" he asked sarcastically.

"She's too scared. Are you?"

"Not in the least."

He balanced his sketchbook & pencil on top of the nearest headstone, then pushed the pram towards the murderer's location.

The ghost girl sat down on the bench. Penny could see the back of her hair was singed and the palms of her hands were scared with burn marks.

"What's your name?" asked Penny.

"Louisa Margaret Foy Wood."

"Nice name. Thank you for warning me, Louisa."

She shook her head and started to sob.

"What's the matter, sweetheart?"

"She's crying because she never had the chance to grow up and make her father proud of her," explained her elderly inner-voice. "As yours is of you."

"How do you know he's proud?"

"It's obvious from the look on his face."

"You can see him?!"

"Yes - he's standing right behind you."

Penny turned around and was just in time to see the ghostly image of her father smiling down at her before it was blotted out by the silhouette of a taller, broad-shouldered man. Even though his features were blacked out, somehow she was certain he had a black spidery birthmark on his left cheek.

He faded away; so she turned her attention back to Louisa.

"Growing up is not all it's cracked up to be," she said, trying to sooth the little girl's sorrow. "I reckon childhood is the best part of life."

"The best part, yes... but not the *only* part!"

"Sorry... I didn't think that through properly."

"That's alright, dear. She knows you were only trying to be kind."

"Is there anything I can do to help her?"

"Yes."

"Name it."

"You can light her a cigarette."

"You're joking?"

"No."

"She's only a child!"

"What harm is it going to do her? She's already dead!"

Penny hesitated for a moment, then took out her lighter and packet of Player's.

Louisa slid to the far end of the bench. "No, please don't!"

"But your other voice said --"

"She knows I hate fire and wants to frighten me!"

She pointed to the headstone Mr. Daniels had left his art gear on. Penny walked over to it and read the inscription:

Sacred to the Memory of
Louisa Margaret Foy Wood.
She departed this life on Thurs. 26th
March, 1840. Aged 11 years.
Her death was occasioned by her apparel
having accidentally taken fire.
The brief period of extreme suffering
which proceeded her dissolution she endured
with Christian fortitude and resignation.
Her uncle, Andrew Ducrow has caused
this tablet to be erected to her memory,
as well as that her final resting place on Earth
may be marked by a memento of her
excellence as in grateful remembrance.

"He must have loved you very much."

She shook her head gravely. "Take her hand and she'll show you," answered her elderly inner-voice.

The second she did, she was standing beside a blazing fireplace. Louisa ran into the room and hid underneath the table. She was obviously terrified.

"What's the matter?" asked Penny.

Louisa couldn't or wouldn't answer her.

A well-dressed man entered and locked the door. "I'm sorry it has to end this way. You've been a good girl; but I can't take the risk of our relationship coming to light." He dragged her out by her ankles and carried her over to the fireplace. "I shall say it was a terrible accident. You stood on the fender to reach for the cutlery on the mantlepiece."

"No, uncle - please! I won't tell anyone. I promise!"

Penny tried to pick up a vase to smash him over the head with, but her hands passed straight through it. She was a future ghost; there to observe - nothing more.

Despite her continued pleading, he held her close to the fire until her crinoline dress was alight... then he let her go and she ran around and around the table screaming until she dropped to the floor engulfed in flames.

Penny closed her eyes. "Please... I don't want to see anymore!" The horrifying warmth of the fireplace was replaced by the comforting coolness of the cemetery. She held Louisa in her arms and they both wept.

The artists arrived back at the bench.

Mr. Daniels retrieved his art gear and began a new pencil portrait.

"Quick girl, fetch me mine!"

Louisa did as she was told and brought Miss Biffen her sketchbook from out of the pram's wheel-rack. With the pencil held between her teeth, and her little helper holding the paper close to her face, the armless artist began her sketch.

"Who are you both drawing? Not me again, surely?"

"No - not you, my dear," answered Mr. Daniels.

"You shall be the judge of which is the best likeness," informed Miss Biffen.

"How will I know?"

When completed, Louisa - to the astonishment of Mr. Daniels: "Dear Lord, my sketchbook is floating in mid-air!" - brought both portraits over to the bench.

Penny felt five eyeballs burrowing into her skull.

They were indeed sketches of someone she knew. They had drawn the black spidery birthmark on his left cheek.

She stood up - letting the sketchbooks slide off her lap - and walked away from the bench. As she passed through the gloomy stone tunnel, the shiver she felt had nothing to do with a 'spooky kind of pleasure' and everything to do with remembered fear.

They had sketched the face of her murderer.

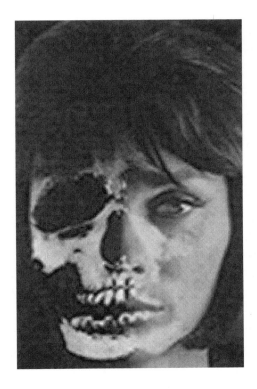

2.

THE GHOSTS OF ST. JAMES' CEMETERY

by Marc Damian Lawler

Location: St. James' Cemetery; fifty feet below street level. Liverpool Anglican Cathedral towering above.

A HARD DAY'S FRIGHT

(Oct. 9th, 1958)

John Lennon pincered the last scallop out of the Falkner Street chippy bag, threw his head back, and lowered it inside his thin-lipped mouth - exhaling a cloud of cold air as he did so. He ran his greasy fingers through his Elvis Presley style quiff - complete with a D.A. (duck's arse) at the back, and shouted to his friend & fellow art student, Stuart Sutcliffe: "Hurry up, Stu. It's bloody freezing down here!"

"Just a mo," Sutcliffe shouted back as he continued to sketch the strange shadows cast by the gathering of gravestones in the corner of the cemetery where the wall was graffitied with the names of long dead stonemasons.

Lennon screwed the bag up into a ball and chucked it over the back of the bench.

Cynthia Powell (her hair dyed blonde to fit in with his fondness for Bridget Bardot) picked it up off the frosty grass and deposited it in the bin on top of Lennon's screwed up artwork.

As she has done every a.m. and p.m. since the Autumn of 1850, Louisa pushed Miss Biffen's pram past the bench that Lennon was lounging on at exactly six minutes to two.

"You're such a goody-two-shoes, Cyn."

"We're in a cemetery, John!"

"Yeah, so? The dead don't mind."

"Actually, we do!"

"Who said that?" asked Lennon, sitting up and looking around.

"I did," answered Miss Biffen.

Cynthia peered inside the pram.

"What's wrong?" asked Lennon, seeing her face drain of colour.

"Nothing. Let's go back to college."

"Who's inside the pram?"

She didn't answer... so he looked for himself.

"Fucking hell, Cyn! No wonder you've turned pale."

"I beg your pardon?!" protested Miss Biffen.

"No offence, love - but you're mingin' to look at!"

"You rude young man!"

"Guilty as charged," he answered, grinning down at her.

Louisa tried to push the pram on, but Lennon blocked her way.

"John, please don't!"

"Shh, Cyn."

"Your mother is very cross with you!" informed Miss Biffen.

"My mother's dead, you stupid cripple!"

"I know she is!"

He was about to push the pram over, but stopped when he heard Julia Lennon's voice: "John, don't you dare!"

His feet turned to stone inside his crepe-soled shoes.

"What's wrong?" asked Cynthia.

"Didn't you hear her?!"

"Who?"

He swallowed hard. "Go and speak to Stu."

"Are you sure?"

"Yeah... Go!"

He waited until she was out of earshot, then asked: "Is she still here?"

"Which one?" answered Miss Biffen, mockingly. "Your down-trodden girlfriend, or your furious mother?"

"Ha, bloody ha!"

"Your mother's gone," answered Louisa.

"Gone? Gone where?!"

"She's..."

"Yes - out with it."

"-- left the cemetery."

He grabbed hold of her arm; ignoring the ice-cold temperature of her skin. "Well then - that means we'll have to go after her."

"That's impossible. We can't leave the cemetery," said Miss Biffen.

"The fuck you can't!"

Keeping a tight grip on the girl's arm, he pushed the pram towards the gloomy stone tunnel.

"How dare you! Stop this instant!" protested Miss Biffen.

"It's your own fault. You shouldn't have told me she was here if you didn't want to follow through with it."

They entered the tunnel... but when Lennon came out at the top he was holding onto and pushing nothing but empty air.

He hurried back down the tunnel.

"Where have your new friends got to?" asked Sutcliffe.

"They vanished."

Stu laughed, but then saw the look of shock on his friend's face and stopped.

"They were ghosts, weren't they, Cyn?"

"Yes, John," she answered with a tremble in her voice.

"I've finished my sketch," said Sutcliffe. "Come on, let's get the hell out of here!"

"No! I have to speak to them again."

He ran back to the bench and kicked over the litter bin. "Come on, you ugly old cripple? Come and tell me off again!"

"John, this is getting you nowhere," reasoned Sutcliffe.

His friend was right - his provocation wasn't working... so he tried a different tactic. He uprighted the litter bin and put the rubbish back in.

"Okay... I'm sorry I talked to you like that. And I'm sorry I grabbed the girl's arm."

Instantly, both ghosts were back beside the bench.

Louisa held out her hand for him to hold. The instant he did, her ghost body changed into his mother's.

"Happy eighteenth birthday, my beautiful boy."

John tried to speak, but was all choked up inside.

Julia smiled at Cynthia.

Although scared, Cynthia smiled back.

"Stay with this one, John. I can sense she's a good girl."

She looked at Sutcliffe and a cloud of sadness passed over her eyes.

"Promise me, you'll keep on with your music."

John nodded.

"And don't trust your dad when he turns up on your doorstep. He'll try and weasel his way back into your life. Don't let him. Send him packin'."

He managed to speak. "It's you I want back, not him!"

Julia took John into her arms and kissed his face. To his relief, she felt warm and real and smelled of her favourite perfume: Moonlight Mist.

She whispered in his ear "Goodbye", and then - in the blink of an eye - she was the ghost girl again.

His initial reaction was to demand his mother's return; but in his heart he knew his time with her was over, so he quickly calmed down.

She pushed the pram on.

"Wait!"

She stopped and looked back and could see the lapels of his leather jacket were shiny with tears.

"Thank you... Sorry, I don't know your name."

"It's Louisa Margaret Foy Wood."

"Thank you, Louisa."

"You're welcome."

"Is there anything I can do for you? Say a prayer or something?"

"When you're famous, will you come back and visit us?"

"Famous - me?!"

"Yes, when you're..." she stopped and thought about it for a moment, " - toppermost of the poppermost!"

"Silly girl. What a dotty thing to say," chided Miss Biffen. "Push on."

(July, 11th 1964)

"Why have you brought us down here, John?" asked McCartney, sleepily.

"Yeah - and at such an ungodly hour," said Harrison between yawns.

"If we'd come down here during the day," explained Lennon. "We'd have been buried under an avalanche of Beatle beasties!"

Starr rubbed his tired eyes and looked up at the high, sandstone walls. "Surely they wouldn't have spotted us all the way down here?"

"Those creepy-crawlies have eyes in the back of their heads!"

"Tut, tut, tut... That's not a nice way to say about our fans," teased McCartney.

Starr lit his last Lark... then dropped the packet onto the grass.

"Pick it up," ordered Lennon.

"Pick what up?"

"The bloody fag packet, of course!"

"Why?"

"Because I said so."

"Arr... Stop picking on Ringo," mocked McCartney.

"Yeah - he's only little," joined in Harrison.

"PICK IT UP!"

Starr did as he was told and stuffed it inside the jacket pocket of his Douglas Millings/Pierre Cardin suit.

"Is that because of the pram lady?" asked McCartney as he dragged himself up off the bench.

"Yeah."

"What pram lady?" asked Harrison as he stretched out.

Neither answered.

"I don't know about you Ringo, but I'm starting to feel left out here."

Starr took a deep drag on his fag and wandered off into the surrounding darkness.

Lennon looked at his wristwatch. It was 1.54 a.m.

They heard Starr talking to someone.

"What are you doing down here so late, love?"

"I'm always here."

"In this cemetery?!"

"Yes."

"Why?"

"Because she's dead," answered Lennon as Louisa came into view.

"She's what?!"

"She's a ghost - as is the old lady in the pram."

"You mean baby?"

"No."

Starr pushed the pram into a patch of moonlight and peered inside... then yelped and ran back to his band mates.

"Is that the drummer?" asked Miss Biffen.

"Yes," replied Louisa excitedly.

"Well, he's the pot calling the kettle black. The sight of his nose alone is enough to make one scream. Where's he gone?"

"He's hiding behind the bench."

"Come out, you big baby!"

"He could say exactly the same to you, love," responded Harrison on Ringo's behalf.

"How dare you! This is my preferred choice of mobility, nothing more."

Louisa parked the pram beside the bench.

"Hello, love. Sorry, I mean - Hello, Louisa."

She beamed up at him. "Can I call you Beatle John?"

"If you like."

"And I'm Beatle Paul," said McCartney, his whole head wreathed in a smile.

Louisa blushed; which is no mean feat for a ghost.

"Pauley, take the pram for a quick spin around the cemetery, will yer?"

"Sure thing, Johnny."

Lennon held out his hand, but Louisa didn't take it.

"I'm sorry, Beatle John. Your mother is not here."

"That's alright. I'm not here to talk to her."

"Who then?"

"My friend, Stuart Sutcliffe. Is he around?"

She thought about it for a moment. "He's on his way."

"On his way? On his way from where?!"

"Hamburg."

"How long is it gonna take him?!"

"Not long, I bet," cut in Harrison. "He's travelling psychically, not physically."

She held out her hand. "He's here."

"That was quick!"

"Told you," said Harrison smugly.

The instant he took hold of her hand he was holding Sutcliffe's.

Stu chuckled as Lennon did his best to turn it into a manly handshake.

"I see you're as reluctant as ever to show your feelings."

"No. I'm just saying hello."

"Oh, OK. Go on then."

"Go on then, what?"

"Say hello."

"Hello, Stu."

"Hello, John."

They laughed and embraced, slapping each other on the back.

"So what's he like?" asked Lennon.

"Who?"

"Buddy Holly."

"Don't know - haven't met him yet."

"So what have you been up to then?"

"I've been hanging out with Astrid in Hamburg."

"Where you there when George and I visited her?"

"I was standing right next to you when she took the photos. We hoped I'd show up when they were developed, but it was just you two."

Harrison was hanging on every word of this ghostly/spiritual encounter.

"Hello, George."

"Hello, Stu. Have you got any better at playing the bass guitar yet?"

"No."

They grinned at each other.

Starr was peering over the back of the bench like a 'Mr. Chad was here' doodle.

"Is Ringo a Beatle now?"

"Yeah," answered John.

"What was wrong with Pete?"

"Nothing much. Ringo fits in better, that's all."

"You mean, he's not as good-looking?"

"I suppose," he admitted.

The moon disappeared behind a patch of cloud making their sombre surroundings appear even more gloomy.

"The answer to your question is... Yes."

"What question?"

"Was it the kick to my head that eventually killed me?"

"Christ, Stu. I'm so sorry."

"Why? It wasn't your fault. You and Pete came to my rescue, remember?"

"Yeah, but if I hadn't asked you to join the band in the first place -"

"Hindsight is a horrible thing, John. It doesn't do any of us much good."

Meanwhile, McCartney had completed half a circuit of the cemetery.

"I'm sure you must be exaggerating," challenged Miss Biffen.

He resolutely shook his mop-top. "Right now, we're the four most popular people on the planet."

"Do you mind putting that to the test?"

"Err... How?"

"When my young helper realised you were here, she sent out a psychic message to all the dead Beatles fans in the city."

"Err... What does that mean?"

She chuckled. "You're about to find out."

He turned the pram around and took a short cut through the headstones.

Starr was the first to hear it - a whirling, rustling, screeching sound; like an army of autumn leaves being tempest tossed towards the cemetery.

"Can you hear that, George?"

Harrison cocked his ear. "It sounds like a ghostly stampede of dead Beatles fans."

"That's exactly what it is!" confirmed McCartney, now back at the bench.

The Fab Three scarpered towards the south end exit.

Lennon remained where he was.

Sutcliffe cut to the chase. "Someone's gonna shoot you, John."

"Shoot me?!"

"Yeah. I don't know when, but I know where - in America."

The whirling, rustling, screeching sound was now circling overhead.

"Jesus, why would anyone want to shoot me?"

"I wish I could tell you more, but that's all I know."

Hundreds of deceased Beatlettes came storming down through the gloomy stone tunnel and into the cemetery with every bit of hysterical determination to get at the Fab Four as their alive counterparts had demonstrated outside the Odeon cinema on London Road only a few hours before at the northern premiere of A Hard Day's Night.

"Bloody Nora!" cried out Lennon as they roared towards the bench. He turned to humour as a way of saying goodbye. "Try to cut back on the Astra beer. You know they give you terrible headaches."

Stu chuckled, appreciating the black humour.

Lennon legged it.

Louisa took back control of her ghost body and pushed the pram out of the way just in time to stop it from being flattened by the spooktacular stampede.

"See? I was right. They are the toppermost of the poppermost."

"It would seem so."

"Did you -"

"Yes, don't worry," she interrupted. "I got the pretty one to sign my sketchbook for you."

"Thank you, Miss Biffen."

"You're welcome, child."

Paul, George and Ringo made it up to street level unscathed, where they scrambled into their chauffeur driven Austin Princess limousine. Lennon was not so lucky. They caught up with him at the foot of the rise and surrounded him in a frenzy of toxic adoration. All he could see was a mess of dead faces - black and blue ones - covered in gore ones - hideously bashed in ones - freakishly white ones - putrefying yellow and green ones; and all of them screaming his name!

The Fab Three hit upon a plan. They got out and heaved open the archway's iron gate; just wide enough for the limousine to fit through.

"Drive down!" ordered McCartney, as soon as their bums were back on the back seat.

"I can't do that. I'll smash into 'em!" protested the chauffeur.

"Don't be daft, fella. They're already dead!"

He drove the limousine up to the gate and shined the headlights down onto the spectral multitude. "Oh, God Almighty!" he said, and fled the vehicle in search of spiritual sanctuary inside the cathedral.

"Cowardly custard!" shouted Starr.

"That's rich coming from you," pointed out Harrison. "You spent most of your time down there cowering behind a bench!"

"Yeah... Well, not any more!" He climbed into the driver's seat and pressed his Cuban heel hard on the accelerator. The limousine roared down the short, steep hill and smashed into the surprisingly solid spectral multitude at the bottom. Blood and puss and God knows what else splashed everywhere.

Starr turned on the wipers; and when the windscreen was clear, they could see Lennon hanging onto the bonnet.

"REVERSE!" he shouted through the glass.

Starr did as he was told and the limousine bumped and rocked its way back up the incline and out through the archway.

As soon as the limousine jerked to a halt, Lennon rolled off the bonnet and dived head-first through the gap created by McCartney flinging open the left-hand side passenger door.

"Thanks, fellas!" he said as he climbed over the back into the front passenger seat. "But how did you know you wouldn't run me over?"

"We didn't," said Starr.

"But that was a chance we were willing to take," added Harrison.

As Starr was turning the vehicle around, several of their from beyond the grave fans - the ones with their arms and legs still attached - suckered themselves onto the outside of the limousine like limpets washed up on a tsunami of pus.

"Can't we have one night off from the constant female attention?" moaned McCartney.

"You've changed your tune," said Harrison. "You're usually the first in line to please the female fans."

"Yeah, but the only thing that lot can attract is flies!"

It didn't take long to shake them off. After a sharp right on Upper Parliament Street, all but a headless hugger were kicked to the kerb. (The fallen evaporated into an early morning mist that floated down to the docks and drifted out over the River Mersey.)

"How can No Head here be so hell-bent on sticking with us, when she can't even see who we are?!" quizzed Lennon.

"Her head is missing, but her eyeballs are psychically present," answered Starr.

"That's a bit clever for you, lad," derided McCartney; although he was obviously impressed.

And Ringo was not yet through with being clever... Eyeing an opportunity for a devilish course of action, he drove the limousine onto the pavement and shish kebabed her rotting body on the arrowhead spike of a wrought iron fence.

Job done. Fag break.

"She's double dead now!" observed Starr as he blew smoke out of the driver's window.

Lennon caught sight of something strange in the rear view mirror and turned around to look. A mist the size and shape of a human head was forming on McCartney's lap.

"Yep, that took care of her alright," enthused McCartney.

"I wouldn't be so sure, Pauley."

"Huh?"

"Look down and you'll see."

McCartney did as Lennon suggested and shrieked like a girl. No head's head was undoing his trouser zip with her teeth!

"Piss in her face. That'll put a stop to her!" suggested Starr.

"I can't! My nether region is frozen with fear!"

"Well, you better do something quick!" warned Harrison. "Before she bites your balls off!"

McCartney stuck his index fingers up her grotty nostrils and lifted her head away from his precious crouch. In response, a long green tongue shot out of her slimy black mouth and wrapped itself around his forearms.

He needed a little help from his friends... Harrison rolled the sparkwheel on his Zippo and started to burn through her tongue; Lennon grabbed hold of her greasy hair and pulled. He heard hissing and half expected to see her hair had morphed into snakes, but it turned out to be the car's overheated engine.

The battle between banshee and Beatles raged on for several minutes until the lighter had completed the job it was being used for, and McCartney's forearms - though covered in green, stinking slime - were free.

"Open the sun roof, Ringo!" instructed Lennon.

Starr pulled a leaver (four years later, it was confirmed - on their sea voyage to Pepperland - that he was a born leaver puller) and with a combined thrust they threw her head up and out of the opening. It rolled off the roof and - would you believe it? - landed on top of her impaled body.

"Aw," sentimentalised Starr. "We've brought about a nice reunion there."

"She'll not be satisfied," said Harrison. "Not after nearly nabbing the ultimate souvenir - a matching pair of Beatle balls."

McCartney shivered and carefully crossed his legs.

"It's dangerous being a Beatle," sympathised Starr.

"Tell me about it," said Lennon; trying in vain not to think about what Stu had said to him.

Meanwhile, back at St. James' Cemetery...

The Beatles late chauffeur (his dicky ticker had called time on him whilst he was beating his fists - to no avail - on the cathedral's locked doors) was staring Death in the face.

The Fab Three had been right to think he'd fled from the limousine out of fear of the dead girls; but what they couldn't possibly have known was... It was out of fear of being recognised by the ones he'd murdered. And the nurse he'd strangled, in that exact location less than two months ago, whilst wearing his black leather driving gloves.

The tall, black, spectral figure that stood before him was no psychopomp version of the Grim Reaper. He - no, SHE - the shroud having blown open to reveal a beautiful female form - scraped the scythe she was clutching in her bony hands against the spidery black birthmark on his left cheek, and with one fell swoop sliced off his manhood.

He was already dead, so the wound didn't bother to bleed; but the searing pain he felt would course through his ghost body for ever.

3.

If a commuter can cope with a little transport terror, who knows where the midnight road might lead to...

Take for example, the young buck in Mr. Sessler's R. Chetwynd-Hayes inspired story...

RED EYE TO NIGHFOLK

by A. P. Sessler

Paul awoke from his short nap with eyes full of sleep and a mouthful of exhaust. By the time he came to his senses the departing Greyhound bus was halfway across the station parking lot.

"No! Wait!" he choked out as he ran after the accelerating vehicle, but it disappeared within seconds. "Dammit!" he shouted and paced, stamping his feet in a path no longer than two yards, even with the length of the entire lot at his disposal.

Despite the shivering cold he pulled his sleeve back to see the wristwatch on his bare, goose-pimpled flesh, as if to convince himself it was some other bus that had just left him alone at the station, but it was 11:52 PM; there was no fooling himself. Completely frustrated, he returned to the bench, this time refusing to sit should he fall asleep, though it made little difference now.

"Dammit, dammit, dammit! Why? Why did you have to fall asleep when you knew the only bus out of here was leaving in 30 minutes? Why, Paul? Why?" he scolded himself and glanced at his watch again, though it did nothing more than make him feel like a complete moron and waste of air - a feeling he was familiar with.

He could already hear his father bitching. "You wouldn't

have missed the bus if you hadn't stayed up all night partying."

The party in question was working until 11 pm.

"You'll never get anywhere in life expecting everyone to give you a handout."

Somehow working two part-time jobs was expecting a handout.

"If you studied harder you wouldn't have a crap job."

Studying harder didn't include his full-time school load crammed between his two jobs.

It made Paul question why he even bothered going home for the holiday. He'd only feel like a stranger, an unwanted one at that, among his own family. There would be hot, mouth-watering food spread across the table and miserable hearts at every seat, making every bite as bland as convenience store fare. Still, there was Mom, the one dim coal in the hearth trying to keep the home fire burning. Why she hadn't left Paul's father was a mystery, but they were traditional people from a traditional time, where you stayed in a marriage no matter how much you suffered. It was her duty to God. First, God, your husband, second, your children, third.

Another reason why he questioned going home. His mother really did love him, but no matter how much she loved him, she would always side with her husband out of duty.

Paul pulled his duffel bag from his shoulder and threw it on the freezing asphalt, its shadow stretched long across the lot by the buzzing fluorescent lights overhead. With a loud huff and a hand through his hair he would rather have put tightly around his neck, he decided to sit down after all.

"Stupid!" he shouted and looked side to side, first wondering if anyone had observed his failure and resulting outburst. Secondly because he could have sworn it was his father's voice he heard and not his own. He quieted down.

"Stupid," he mumbled to himself.

A sound directed his attention to the far side of the lot.

A bus? And from what he saw - if he saw it - someone had just boarded and the folding doors had just shut. But his bus was the last one out that night. He pulled the ticket out of his pocket to remind himself: DEPARTURE TIME, 11:45 PM.

"Last ride out of town," he said and returned the ticket to his pocket, then looked at the bus. "So what is that?"

He took his bag and crossed from the well-lit waiting area to the place where sky and tarmac bled black into one another.

The rumbling engine and plumes of blue-white exhaust meant the bus was just arriving or about to leave.

He knocked on the door then leaned close to peer inside, but it was difficult to see through the tinted glass. When no one answered he knocked again. A moment later the door swished open.

The driver sat in the dark, a minimum of his features illuminated by the glowing controls of the dashboard. "Can I help you?" he said.

Paul smirked. "You heading to Dayton by any chance?"

The driver rolled his eyes in a full circle. "We'll be passing through. But we're full."

"Great. So you can get me there?"

"Like I said, we're filled to capacity."

Paul glanced at the row of tinted windows along the bus.

"It's alright. I'll stand. I just need a ride, like tonight, right now," he said, but already knew he was testing the driver's patience. He opened his wallet and pulled out a number of bills. "Please, man. I'll give you every cent I got on me."

The driver's chest swelled. "Can't do it. It's the rules," he said and gripped the handle to close the doors.

Paul stepped onto the stair. "No, wait! Please. You can make an exception."

The driver's hand rested on the handle. "I could lose my job. Besides, I can't ask my passengers to-"

"Let him on," a masculine voice called from one of the seats.

Paul beamed with hope. "See? He doesn't mind."

The driver flashed someone a nasty glance. "Look, I really don't think-"

"No, really. We don't mind," said another voice.

The driver sighed and the leather wheel groaned beneath his tightening grip.

A woman's voice cooed. "He sounds absolutely deli-"

"Okay, alright. Enough already. He can ride," the driver said and threw another nasty look before facing Paul with a nod.

"Looks like it's unanimous. You win by a landslide. Come on."

"Thank you so much. Thank you all, really," Paul said and stepped up through the open door. He offered the driver the wad of cash. "Here you go."

The driver glanced at the fold of bills, tempted a moment to keep it all, but after a momentary bout with his conscience, he counted them, stuffed a few in the fare box, and handed Paul his change.

"Oh, that's not-" Paul started when the driver caught his wrist.

"Necessary? Of course, it's not. I don't want it said I ever took advantage of anyone," the driver said, his voice low and harsh as the biting wind at Paul's back. He pressed the bills hard into Paul's palm and shoved his hand away.

Paul wasn't sure whether to thank the driver or give him a

piece of his mind, but before he could decide the door had shut, leaving the wind to howl outside like a dog left in the cold.

He faced the aisle and noticed for the first time it was completely dark, and it only grew more so as the bus went into gear and pulled past the brightly-lit station onto the dark highway.

He held a hand above his brow, as if the dark should become less. "Sure is dark."

"Yep," said the driver. "Now go on, find your seat. You can't stand the whole ride."

Are we back on speaking terms? Paul wanted to ask, but after a glance at the back of the driver's head he assumed they weren't.

"No, really. Why is it so dark?" Paul asked no one in particular.

"Lion's Club," said a soft, clear voice somewhere ahead, maybe to his left.

Somewhere farther came a laugh.

"What's that?" Paul asked, stepping deeper into the dark.

"Yes," someone agreed, off to Paul's right. "We're visually impaired you see."

Another laugh, to the left.

"See?" said a voice behind him.

Paul looked over his shoulder. It was just as dark behind, except for the glow of the gauges on the dashboard and the lit road ahead. Something inside told him to look to the floor. He remembered that airplanes and public transit had to keep the aisle illuminated.

"It's the rules," he almost heard the driver say.

Small orange rectangles of light lined the floor, but they became a blur the further ahead he looked, which only served to remind him to stop putting off his visit to the eye doctor. He continued toward the back of the bus.

Without his sight to aid him he was left to rely solely on touch, so he put his hands forward and slowly spread them apart until his fingertips brushed the cool of leather seat cushions.

He ran his left hand from the cushion toward the front of the bus, until he felt a scratchy tweed suit.

"Pardon me," Paul said to the stranger.

"No worries," came a soft voice.

Paul repeated the motion to his right. The warm flesh of a bare neck or back. "I'm sorry," he said, his voice going high.

"Not at all," a woman's voice cooed.

Paul's stomach turned at the thought of a shrivelled old woman with ghastly pale eyes wanting him. He stepped forward, not even sure if he had cleared the row of seats. His right hand was arcing forward when he caught a wiry beard. "Please, forgive me."

A grunt.

He turned sharply.

"Watch it!" a voice said, but Paul was sure he hadn't touched anyone.

He took another step, hopeful he wouldn't catch another face. His left hand tried the seat, inched forward, and found an unusual texture. Ridged, plastic. A woman's purse?

"Do you mind?" came an offended voice, high, its gender indistinguishable.

"I'm so sorry," Paul said. Even in the pitch black he imagined his face was red enough to be seen. He continued toward the back, issuing this statement: "Everyone, I do apologize. I'm hav-

BEFORE YOU BLOW OUT THE CANDLE...

ing trouble finding a seat. If someone could just direct me to the nearest available..."

A hand grabbed his wrist; hairy and sweaty. Paul's heart nearly came out his mouth.

"Have a seat," said a man.

"Where?"

"Beside me. It's a window seat, if you don't mind."

What choice did Paul have? "Not at all," he said and squeezed past the man. "Sorry," he apologized again, sure he had put his ass square in the man's face.

"No need," said the man. "Tight quarters."

Paul chuckled. "No doubt," he said and took his seat, holding the bag in his lap. "Thank you so much, I really do appreciate it."

"It's no problem. We all need a helping hand sometime.

Someone to look out for us. Wouldn't you agree?" said the man, but Paul could only think of the hairy, sweaty hand that had taken his wrist. His flesh still felt damp, but maybe it was his imagination, made all that more active in his present environment.

"Istan," said the man with an accent Paul couldn't rightly place; something oddly European or plainly Middle-Eastern.

"I'm sorry?" said Paul.

"My name. Istan."

"Oh. Paul," he said, dreading that the moist hand was now extended and waiting his own.

Reluctantly he reached out and found it. They shook. The large hand nearly swallowed his, and speaking of swallow, it should be noted the hand really was quite sweaty, almost as if salivating.

"Nice to meet you, Paul."

"Same here, Istan."

"And tell me, Paul. What brings one out in the middle of night, on a bus full of-"

"Visually impaired people?" Paul volunteered, suddenly conscious that the term 'blind' might be offensive.

Istan laughed. "Yes, visually impaired."

"Can I ask something?"

"Yes. Speak freely."

"If no one can see, why are you on a bus with no lights?"

There was a soft "Hmm," a confirmation that seemed to assure Paul it was a legitimate question. "Surely you are aware that those well acquainted with darkness have by nature learned to rely on their other senses, which over time become quite attuned."

"Oh yeah. Sure."

"Fluorescent lighting," Istan pointed to the ceiling, though Paul certainly couldn't see. "The kind commonly in convenience stores or shopping centers, produces a most unpleasant buzz that becomes nearly unbearable after the shortest period. As you can imagine being forced to sit in a confined space such as this for any amount of time would practically drive one mad, don't you think?"

"I hadn't thought about it like that. Yeah, I guess so."

Then again, wouldn't staring into the darkness for hours on end do the same? What a miserable existence, Paul thought when considering the lot of those surrounding him. I'd rather be dead.

He stared into the darkness, his eyes darting side to side in search of meaning, definition to the blur of shapes before him that may or may not have been chiseled and conjured from the pixels of light generated by his overcompensating rod cells.

"Just imagine you're camping out in the woods," suggested Istan, his shoulder brushing Paul's as he leaned close.

Paul swallowed uncomfortably. "It would be easier if I were trying to fall asleep."

"Go ahead. No one will mind."

"I can't. I'm wide awake."

"Perhaps I can help."

Paul thought of the joke and laughed before he delivered the punchline. "You going to sing me a lullaby?"

"Look here," said Istan, and without questioning, without reasoning that in the very pitch black he could see nothing, Paul faced him, and saw a pair of glowing red eyes.

Paul jumped half out of his seat.

"Nightmare?" Istan inquired.

Paul turned, expecting to find the demonic red peepers staring back, but only darkness sat before him. His rapid breathing pierced the steady hum of the bus engine.

"Everything alright?" an airy voice came from over his shoulder, accompanied by foul, dank breath and the squeak of leather upholstery.

"Our friend had a bad dream," said Istan.

"Oh, those are the best kind," the man said and patted Paul's shoulder. "Good for you."

Another squeak followed, presumably the man leaning back into his seat.

"I swear I was just awake," said Paul.

"You were, as I believe they say, 'sawing the logs'. No worries. We all have nightmares from time to time. They're but messages from the soul."

"But I don't remember falling asleep," Paul insisted.

"Welcome to never-ending darkness," said Istan. "Consider it a form of jet lag. You will adjust in time."

Another squeak.

"Perhaps Almara can whip you up something," said the man from behind, his breath turning Paul's stomach sour.

"I think our friend will be fine," said Istan. "Won't you?"

Paul passed gas. "Excuse me. I have to use the bathroom," Paul said and stood slowly so not to stir the pot roiling in his guts.

There was a dull knock when his head met the overhead compartment. "Ow!" he complained.

"Mine your head," said the stinking voice from behind.

"No kidding," Paul said and placed his bag in his seat.

"Pardon, Istan."

"Just a moment," Istan said, his legs brushing against Paul's as he turned them aside.

"Thank you," Paul said and squeezed past him into the aisle.

The orange lights lining the floor were a steep pyramid amid a black sky, one he began to scale to its very summit, past the grunts, groans, smells and crude remarks of his fellow passengers.

If only I had a light, he thought, when it occurred to him he did. He took the cell phone from his pocket and unlocked the screen with a swipe of his finger.

The icons were practically blinding. After a moment he found the Flashlight app, finger-clicked it and aimed his phone forward to reveal a stern-faced woman standing before him, her hair pinned back in a tight bun and her long, plain dress most conservative. She looked to be of some strict religious order:

Pentecostal, Quaker, Amish - they all looked the same to him.

"Pardon me," he said with a nervous laugh and gazed into her face for long enough a moment for it to seem rude to a sighted person; expecting some acknowledgement of his presence.

She clearly hadn't done so or she would have moved, but when he saw her pale, unblinking eyes, his blood ran cold. His fingers trembled, skid across the screen, and the phone went dark.

"Just gonna squeeze past you," he said, his voice cracking as he made himself narrow with a pivot of his heel. When he advanced, the very thought of her haunting eyes turned the air to ice. "Nice meeting you," he mumbled, if only out of good humor to calm his nerves.

He raised the phone to his eyes to find the Flashlight app only to see the Battery icon blink its last flicker of life and out it went, plunging him back into darkness once more.

Great. Now I'm blind, he thought, then felt incredibly guilty for handling a temporary loss of sight so inadequately.

Back to fumbling about, he extended his hands and continued to the summit of the neon pyramid where he arrived at last. His fingers traced the wall to the corner, and turning to his left they found the hairline crevice separating wall from door.

Starting with small circles that spiralled into bigger circles, he eventually found the handle to the restroom door and gave it a jiggle.

From behind the door the muffled voice sounded nothing like English, but presumably the translation was OCCUPIED.

His stomach continued to churn. He passed gas. Somebody coughed.

A soft creak and strong stench announced the door had opened. He stepped back to avoid the form which exited with a grunt Paul took to mean "Pardon me"; or perhaps "Sorry about the John. You got a match?"

There was a swift draft as the man returned to his seat, as if an 18-wheeler had passed by, which made Paul picture a man of enormous size. The floor of the bus stated as much with groan after groan beneath the man's heavy footsteps, alongside cough after cough from the overpowering stink that followed him.

"I was beginning to think you fell in," said a woman, followed by another grunt-grunt-something. "Perhaps Almara can whip up something for your tum-tum."

Whoever Almara was, hopefully she could whip up something for everyone else, like a gas mask. Paul was tempted to leave the door open. Who would see? And after that stink filled the bus, who would notice? Except his stomach was in knots and there would be loud, audible fireworks of the gastric variety.

He pulled the door shut, undid his pants and sat on the toilet seat in the pitch black restroom, holding his breath as long as he could.

His first thought was "It's dry. Thank God." His second was "Nice of him to warm up the seat", and his third was - upon gasping for air - "Oh God, it stinks so bad!"

It turned out to be a blessing in disguise, for it loosened his bowels, allowing him for a quick and thorough evacuation, but then a new problem arose: how would he know when it was done wiping? What if he sat around the rest of the ride with swamp ass like Mr. Swamp Ass himself? Would Almara whip up a cure for that, too?

He suddenly became aware the bus has stopped. The vibration was different, implying the engine was still running.

Like his fellow passengers, he was becoming attuned to his other senses amid the constant darkness.

There were voices outside. Raised and muffled. Agitated.

Were blind people about to get into a brawl? Paul reached for his cellphone.

I gotta record this, he thought. Wait, your battery is dead. Besides, it's dark, stupid. And lastly - Wash your hands before you touch that thing, man!

He found the sink and soap easy enough; washed his hands and stepped from the restroom into a blinding ray of light.

"Hold it right there!" a man shouted from behind the flashlight beam blazing fire into Paul's eyes. "Why aren't you dressed for the party like your friends here?"

"Excuse me? What party?" said Paul, shielding his eyes from the one thing he so desperately wanted the entire ride up until this moment.

"The Halloween party," the man said as he illuminated the passenger's faces for Paul to see.

Among those highlighted were a hairy, tiny-horned devil... a curly-horned satyr somewhere across the aisle... a leathery-skinned reptilian with flicking tongue... a green-skinned witch in black with pointy hat... an old gray man wearing the same, but in blue, covered in strange silver symbols... a giant hairy thing that looked half-ape (surely Mr. Swamp Ass himself); seated next to a little hag of a woman with matted hair full of twigs... and lastly a stately man in cape with slick black hair - both he and the devil thing shared the same blood-red eyes.

What struck Paul odd was that all the blind party guests had trained their eyes (their unseeing eyes?) upon him, and wicked smiles instantly formed upon what appeared to be very articulate masks - too articulate. Paul's attention shot to the driver, who immediately turned forward in his seat and pulled his cap down over his eyes.

The devil thing stood, now spotlighted, beside what Paul realized was the only empty seat; surely Istan himself.

"Apologies for our deception, Paul. You've been a most patient guest, but now, if you will, return to the restroom, or else close your eyes. You do not wish to see this," he said and faced another passenger. "Ladine," he said and a woman arose from her seat, the beam focusing on her.

The church girl Paul had almost walked into floated towards the flashlight and the man behind it, who he now recognized as a policeman.

"Ma'am, please stay in your seat," he said and she passed right through him, eliciting audible shivers and chattering teeth and the complete drainage of his flashlight battery with her freezing, ghostly presence, just as she had Paul's cellphone.

In the flashes of blue and red bleeding through the bus's windows, Paul saw the man's horrified face, frozen in his memory and time like a drama mask. Paul retreated into the restroom and turned the lock to shut out the world dark and black with its screams all bloody red.

The bus was moving again, evidenced by the rattling mirror and toilet seat. Paul was no longer sure if he was awake or dreaming, but whatever it was, it was a nightmare. Or what did Istan call it? A message from the soul? No thanks, thought Paul.

A rap came on the door. His head spun to face what he couldn't see.

"Paul?" said Istan.

Paul didn't answer, as if he could fool the very one who told him to take refuge in the restroom. He shook his head.

"Go away."

"We won't hurt you," said Istan.

"I'm supposed to believe a bunch of..." What were they anyhow?

"Monsters?" said Istan. "Yes, believe a bunch of monsters."

For certainly you realize any number of us could tear this door from its hinges, if not pass straight through it if we so choose."

Paul hadn't considered such a thing, but Istan's words rang true; so he swallowed his fear and opened the door.

"Do not fear," Istan said, his hand finding the small of Paul's back. "It is an unnecessary waste."

Istan led Paul toward their seats. Halfway there Paul lost his footing on something slippery.

"Anna Lee, I told you to clean that up," said Istan.

"Sssorry, Issstan," a feminine voice hissed, and in the darkness something whipped and slurped, followed by a satisfied "Mmm, that'sss sssso good."

"Much better," said Istan, and with a few more steps pushed Paul into his window seat.

Paul hyperventilated.

"Relax," said Istan.

"Eas... Easy for you to say."

Paul struggled to get out, but was trapped between something that looked like the devil - if not the Devil himself - and a window, on a bus, in the dark.

"You are fortunate to see the things you have - the things you will - and live to tell about them."

"Who would believe me?"

A laugh. "Precisely. We hide in doubt like you sit now in darkness. Is it not poetic?"

Paul rubbed sweating palms on his legs, forgetting a devilish hand sat on his left. When their flesh met, he winced.

"Do not fear," Istan reminded him. "We will leave you be. It is not often we have a comrade of your kind, such as our dear driver."

Paul looked to the dimly lit face in the rear view mirror.

Their eyes met momentarily.

"Yes. He has been a faithful companion for many years now. In fact, I will let you in on a secret: he probably doesn't know himself how many years he's been our driver. He's over a century old. It was the least I could do for his service."

Paul faced Istan. "What are you going to do with me?"

Istan squeezed his thigh and chuckled. "My dear Paul, do not concern yourself with such matters. The future is not yours to see, only to accept."

"Is that what you said to him?" Paul said, gesturing toward the driver. "Told him not to worry and now he's your eternal chauffeur?"

"He is well compensated. Weekends off. He never gets sick, never grows old. And he has his fill of women. He is amply satisfied in all things."

"Except he's your slave."

"Is your work so different, yet so less rewarding?"

Damn. That hurt.

The bus came to a stop. The doors opened.

"Dayton, last stop before Nighfolk," the driver announced.

Paul didn't move, even when Istan's hand left his thigh.

"I believe this is your stop," said Istan.

Was it? Paul looked through the tinted window, and for the first time in hours he saw light; not a blinding or moving beam swallowed in an instant by ghosts, or flashing blue and red, but an entire platform of cold metal benches and double glass doors, all brightly-lit, and in between he and the station his own reflection, and over his shoulder, Istan's glowing eyes.

Paul imagined his homecoming again. Warm table. Cold hearts. Father criticizing every single thing about him.

Mother acquiescing. A sister and brother equally defeated.

Their only hope of escape the death of their patriarch, or fleeing for sanity.

Back in the city: work. Endless work at jobs that didn't provide, and an education he knew in his heart wouldn't grant him an ounce of the freedom he desired.

Beside him: darkness, death, or was it evil? Pure evil. At any rate something unnatural. Something unknown.

"Last stop before Nighfolk," the driver repeated.

"Paul?" Istan prodded.

Paul's body tensed. Every muscle said Stand. Get off the bus. Run! But something else spoke to him; deeper still. Something within reach. Obtainable. And it welcomed him without reservation, expectations or judgement.

Beneath the red eyes reflected over his shoulder a gleaming white smile of pointed teeth appeared. "You will be joining us then?"

Paul couldn't believe his eyes and ears. He saw his reflection nod and his mouth open and say: "Yes, I think I will."

"Driver, our friend wishes to continue to Nighfolk." Istan spoke for everyone to hear.

An excited chorus of whispers rose from all around. A hand found Paul's shoulder from behind. "Very good, friend. Very good indeed!"

Paul's stomach didn't heave at the man's horrendous breath. He even turned to face the man, and now, somehow, through the dark, he saw the squat, little man and his round, fat face covered in warts, his drooping eyelids nearly concealing his glazed hazel eyes.

43

Paul placed his hand upon the man's. "Yes, sir. It'll be a good journey. Very good."

As the bus continued down the dark road to Nighfolk, a peculiar, yet not disagreeable song rose from the passengers. Even though Paul had never heard such a strange tune, or such weird words, they felt familiar and, like Istan's words, rang entirely true. So he raised his voice high and sang along with the motley crew of monsters he now considered friends.

4.

'In 2010, a modern-day treasure hunter was browsing through an antique shop in Fresno, California. Flipping through boxes, he came across an old photograph of an unsmiling group of men playing croquet in front of a wooden building in a rural setting. He paid $2 for it and walked out.

After much investigation, it was concluded that one of the men was Billy the Kid, a.k.a. Henry McCarty, and the other players were his gang, The Regulators. It was only the second known photograph of the Wild West's most infamous outlaw, and it was worth several million dollars.' --- Richard Davis, An Introduction to Collecting Vintage Photographs.

Just like the proprietor of the antique shop in Fresno, the protagonist in Mr. Gonzalez's tale has no idea of the importance of a photograph in his possession. Although it is worth only pin money, it is rich in paranormal significance to a collector of occult photography.

FEAR MAKES GOOD MATERIALISTS

by Lemuel Caleb Gonzalez

Albert Wheedle, a spongy man with a ruddy face, sat opposite Cabal in the café, at the pedestal table with unsteady foot. He was beaming with cheerful expectancy, nodding and winking at anyone making eye contact; the waitress, the other customers, his reflection in the cutlery. Cabal, for this reason, ignored him, fixing his full interest on a half dozen color photographs laid out on the tabletop between his abandoned tart and Wheedle's iced coffee. Cabal was not a friendly man, and his appearance was intimidating: dark, lofty, with a spring-knife spine.

"A little financial contribution? You wouldn't mind that, would you Mr. Cabal? I appreciate the coffee, and we can call that the price of the showing. Now, given your unusual area of interests, as Mr. Hare described them, I thought you would want to add this to your collection. I am not asking for a large sum, just a donation to keep me in small comforts? Cigarettes are expensive, at least my brand is."

Wheedle's gestures were small and pleading, even to the timid smile that pulled up the corners of his mouth under his pudding cheeks. A stark contrast to Cabal. There was no rigidity to him. An anatomical examination might reveal a flimsy stalk sprung from his sedentary hips to support his acquisitive brain.

"How did they come into your possession?" asked Cabal, curtly.

"In one of Edward Hare's books! Hare's Books is a stop I make to stretch out the best part of my day, the part before I get home to an empty apartment. That is the other minor expense that pleases me: books. I don't know how to do much more than please myself, so that should be my main occupation. Now, if we can come to an agreement..."

Wheedle tampered anxiously with his napkin, hoping his fussing would distract Cabal's attention from the snapshots. It did not.

"I suppose that my personal calamities aren't important," Wheedle grumbled, breaking character accidentally.

Cabal started to sort the pictures according to theme and content.

"The book?" asked Cabal.

Wheedle produced an octavo, with embossed laurels on the boards.

"It was tucked into what Edward Hare called a 'conjugate leaf.' I don't know why I decided to look at this particular book, but it was in the discount shelf where I get all of my library. It was probably the title that got my attention, The Night Side of Nature. It sounded like a book about animals. I like animals. Have you read The Wind in the Willows? Very entertaining! Well, this book was about horrible things, not at all entertaining. Still, it was very compelling, all of those ghosts and demons... compelling but terrible. I can't stop reading it. I'm sure the kind of person who would read such a book is certainly the kind of person who would keep those pictures."

Cabal looked up from the photographs momentarily to the book. Then he returned to his collation.

"There is something else, Wheedle?"

"Oh! The postcard! I've been using it as a bookmark."

"I need to see it."

"I'll lose my place!"

Cabal snapped his fingers impatiently. Wheedle hurried the postcard from the pages of his book, replacing it with a napkin.

The postcard presented a weird nocturnal landscape of black basalt raised up in saw-toothed hackles, and half-healed volcanic vents grizzled with creosote and saguaro cactus. An impossibly large moon filled the sky. There were no structures or figures in the landscape to give scale, and the pearly light made for strange perspectives.

"It doesn't look real, does it?" asked Wheedle.

"It is. The caption identifies this scene as the Sonoran desert, a strange and lonely place. Wild, sudden thunderstorms, chaparral spontaneously bursting into flames, venomous reptiles, spiders the size of your tea saucer. There are petroglyphs left behind by mysterious prehistoric peoples. A strange place, that desert."

"I didn't think the postcard was important. I mean that, it is really the one photograph..."

"All of the photographs, and the postcard, are important. They tell a story when taken together. You are correct in assuming that there is a connection between the book and these images. I would imagine that someone, having taken these photographs, bought this second hand copy of a book on psychic phenomena; clairvoyance, diabolism, to try to understand what it meant. Not an ideal selection to help with understanding this kind of experience, but it was probably what she could lay her hands on. Now, the postcard provides me with the most valuable information."

Cabal pointed to the first photograph in the sequence as he had arranged them, descending toward him. It featured a pair of pretty young women, one with short curly hair, and another with bangs. They sat together in one armchair, in each other's arms.

"This photograph," said Cabal, "has a date stamp on the reverse side. The date follows the postmark on the card by twelve days. Together they put the time of our story at about thirty years ago. If I were of a less reclusive inclination I could have guessed that by their hair, or clothing. Judging from the superficial resemblance between the two women, and the intimacy they share, they are related. Sisters, as we will see."

Cabal lifted the postcard and read the reverse aloud:

Dear Hazel,

I thought you should see where I spent so much time this summer. You will love it here. It's all so beautiful! You will love the primrose and verbena in the garden, the quail strutting across the driveway, and stargazing in the old boneyard outside Oatman. Looking forward to your visit.

Love to Enos,

Beth.

This was delivered in Cabal's harsh staccato, lacking any sympathy or affection.

"This is written by Ms. Beth Mills to her older sister," Cabal continued, tapping the faded image of the older sister in the first photograph, "Hazel Lurton. Hazel visits her, and Beth arranges some kind of reception."

Cabal pointed out the second photograph, showing a spindly man with a smiling face, limbs hooked at awkward angles, while Beth cheered in the background.

"This is evidence of dancing - or, perhaps, some kind of medical emergency."

Wheedle was pleased at the photograph. Looking on others enjoying themselves, without his participation, was a long standing habit.

"It looks like they are having a good time. I wonder what they were dancing to?"

"If they are having a 'good time' is irrelevant!" said Cabal, peevishly. "Now, this photograph shows that the occasion spilled out of doors, and from appearances this is the 'bone-yard' mentioned in the postcard. An abandoned graveyard. You see the grave-markers in disrepair? It has ceased to function as consecrated ground and become an entertainment destination for feckless young people. Now, judging from the eyes and slack faces, and perhaps the quality of the dancing, they are drunk."

Cabal pointed out the next three photographs, showing the sisters accompanied by a young man, a small, pretty blonde, and two others who refused to turn to the full view of the photographer for the rest of the succession.

"Now this -" said Cabal with keen enthusiasm, "is the most interesting photograph."

"And the most valuable?" asked Wheedle, earnestly.

"It appears to have been taken with no awareness of its exceptional content."

"So it's a good example of this kind of trick photography, right? Good enough to pay for? Hare said you had a huge collection on religion, the occult, and metaphysics. This is an example of, 'spirit photography', right? Those things made with double exposures and clip art pictures? Now, can we finally discuss money? It would help me if I could name an amount and you could agree..."

"You are assuming that this is a fake?"

"It can't be authentic," whispered a shocked Wheedle.

"Authentic?" That depends. In that it is genuine? Yes. It most certainly is genuine. It is a part of this sequence of photographs. The image is not caused by a defect in the camera, as the pictures before and after it show no distortions. Neither do they show atmospheric conditions that could account for it."

"So then, this picture shows something that was there at the time. An actual thing?"

"In some sense, Mr. Wheedle, yes. Not an actual object in the way you think. Not like a fencepost or a parked automobile, but a thing. The fact that no one in the photograph seems to be aware of this manifestation is certainly suggestive."

"What if it was something caught in the lens? That could create an... this illusion?"

"That would not account for the amount of detail. See this..."

"I don't like looking at it."

Cabal gave Wheedle a look of intense scorn. Wheedle, shamed, pulled the photograph in question toward him.

The picture showed the happy sisters in flash bulb light. Beth was reduced to a blurry miniature, while Hazel, in focus, appeared much larger. Between the two hung a pale, ragged smear, torn and pitted in a way that suggested a withered face. Despite the absence of actual eyes to communicate intention, it seemed to be regarding Beth maliciously. It was faintly luminous, mottled with objects that could be seen through it.

"Does it bother you, Mr. Wheedle? Fear makes good materialists. If you accept that beings like this lurk, largely unseen, you will never be able to sleep easy again. Every dark closet, or quiet room, is its hunting ground, every human soul is its preferred prey. Not only in some abandoned place, but in your own home."

Wheedle turned away from the horrible image.

"All right, just take the damned thing. I don't want it. I'll only throw it away. The picture is disturbing. A disturbing fake. I've heard about photographs like this before. They usually turn out to be fakes. Misidentification or hoaxes."

"Most of the time," said Cabal. "Then there are other occasions. On those occasions the explanation is that someone photographed a ghost."

5.

Chiaroscuro (from Italian - chiaro, "light" - scuro, "dark") is a technique employed in the visual arts to represent light and shadow as they define three-dimensional objects. But Shutterbug Sadie - the heroine in Mr. Hodson's story - doesn't just photograph sunlight and shadows on her Polaroid camera, she captures (or does it capture her?) what light and darkness symbolise to the human eye manifested as real.

CHIAROSCURO

by Brad C. Hodson

The church had the look of something ancient. Though wooden, its chipped and faded paint, perhaps originally white, but now gray, recalled the giant stones that jutted from the hillside when Daddy took her hiking. It was as though it had always been here, and the forest had simply grown around it.

The building was nearly identical to an old pioneer church her class had visited on a field trip. That structure had been restored and maintained while this one forgotten. Yet the squat, single story with arched windows running along its length was of the same construction. The steeple rising over the door to claw at the canopy of tree limbs overhead may have been taller than that of the restored church, but the basic design was the same. The village they had visited was meant to teach them about Tennessee pioneers in the late 1700s. Could this church be so old?

Strange, then, that it wasn't more of a ruin. The windows, while permanently fogged and smeared, were intact. The walls showed no visible signs of rot or collapse. Even the double-doors on the entrance hung perfectly from their hinges. No kudzu climbed the church and, to the best she could see, no birds nested here. She didn't understand how something so old could be in such good condition without anyone caring for it.

Kudzu did cover the fence surrounding it, however. Three feet high, it was difficult to tell whether it was wood or metal thanks to the green swallowing it. It was as though the earth itself had risen up to create a barrier around the place.

Rain tapped a lazy rhythm against the trees around her. The morning's storm had hurried past, filling puddles and blowing leaves around before continuing on. It left behind gray skies and tired drops of precipitation brushed about by a cool breeze. She loved the forest like this, and especially at this time of year, that borderland between winter and spring when the ice and snow had been banished and the trees, bare and gray for so long, sprouted green in erratic bursts. The air was not yet warm, and no flowers bloomed, but late February in East Tennessee was what Mama called "a little slice of Heaven."

She had been the one to suggest Sadie trek out here. Not across the creek, of course. Nor to the church, undiscovered until now. But Mama knew the girl could not stomach watching her when the tremors came, or the coughing fits that had been so rare this time last year but now visited with alarming frequency. With a smile still vibrant despite how thin her face had become, eyes sparkling beneath a now hairless brow, Mama had told her to take her Christmas present outside and snap a picture of something fantastic.

"With the rain letting up," she'd struggled to say, "you may find some lizards running about. Maybe some crawdads at the creek, if it didn't overflow." Her voice had grown hoarse and strained over the last month. "You might even..."

A braying cough had interrupted her, wracking her body with such violence that the blanket on her lap fell to the floor and Sadie worried she might tumble from the wheelchair.

She rushed to Mama and rubbed her back, the muscles there tense with every cough, the outline of her spine visible through her shirt. The ridges bowed up from her back with such definition that the girl wondered how there was anything left of her other than sharp angles of bone.

"You need anything, Mama? Water? Want me to turn on the humidifier?"

Mama waved the suggestions away as the coughing subsided. "Just slide on those rain boots and get your jacket. If you hurry, you might get me a picture of a rainbow. When I was a girl, my favorite thing after it rained was to find a spider web - one of them big ones they stretch between two trees. Those webs gather fat drops of rain on them. Look like rhinestones. If the light hits them just right, they shine and sparkle. Sometimes you get little rainbows in the webs, even."

Sadie fought the last boot on and stood, stomping on the floor for good measure. "That sounds pretty, Mama."

Mama took her hand. "If you see one, you get me a picture of it."

She felt the tremors in her mother's fingers. Not bad. Not now, anyway. They would worsen.

Daddy came in from the garage, wiping his massive hands on an oil-stained rag. "Where you think you're going?"

"She's going out to play in the rain," Mama said.

"Like Hell."

"Earl."

"How you expect me to finish that wheelchair ramp in the garage if she ain't here to look after you and Booger?"

"The baby's taking a nap," she said, still referring to Nicky as a baby even though he had turned four in January. "And don't call him Booger. You know how I hate that."

He smiled. "Sorry. Just slips out."

Sadie knew her father's cousins had all called him Booger when he was a kid. She didn't know why but, being a kid herself, could guess. Sadie had somehow dodged that particular bullet, but Nicky hadn't been so lucky. For the entirety of her little brother's life, Mama had been asking Daddy to stop using the nickname. Daddy would always smile and apologize, though Sadie suspected he never had any intention of stopping.

"Let the girl out of the house, Earl." Mama pulled her hand back from Sadie, the shaking growing stronger as she placed it on her lap. "It's Saturday. An eleven-year-old girl should be out there playing, not in here practicing nursemaid."

Daddy bent and lifted the blanket from the floor. Replacing it on Mama's lap, he covered her trembling hands. Then he leaned in and kissed the top of her head. His dark hair had grown shaggy over the past few weeks and fell into his eyes. As he stood, he brushed it back with an irritated swipe. Mama had been telling him to get a haircut, but he hadn't had the time. If he wasn't at work, he was taking Mama to the doctor, or helping Sadie with her homework, or fixing the thousand little things around the house that had only been minor annoyances before Mama got sick but now troubled him with a desperate urgency. The purple circles under his eyes showed how even sleep had become a luxury he just could not work into his schedule.

"All right," he said and turned to Sadie. "You get. Just don't be gone too long. I need you to help me with supper later."

Sadie slid her backpack on and grabbed her Christmas present, an old Polaroid Sun 600 Daddy had found at the flea market. He traded for the camera, purchasing it for the low price of his father's Oak Ridge Boys albums, one Conway Twitty 8-track, and a silver lighter with a faded wolf forever howling on its side. The Polaroid came with a black leather carrying case she wore around her neck and two dozen boxes of film. His boss at the plant had told him that when the film ran out or the flash stopped working, he could find more on the internet. Daddy had never been much for computers, but Sadie had gone online at school and confirmed that. Knowing it did not make her less cautious about what she used her film on, however.

"Why not just take pictures with your cell phone?" Casey Longren asked when Sadie bragged about the camera at school.

"It's not the same," Sadie said, not willing to admit that she couldn't afford a phone. Even if she had one, she would have stuck with the Polaroid. She wasn't quite able to articulate the magic she found in the white-bordered photographs the machine produced, but knew it to be special.

She snapped a photograph of Mama before she left, her mother laughing and holding up a hand in protest. Sadie slid it into her pocket to develop, kissed Mama on the cheek, and punched Daddy in the arm, sprinting out the door before he could catch her with retaliatory tickles.

Sadie had wanted to find the perfect photograph for Mama, but after half an hour had found nothing worthy of her film. She had followed the creek as it wound through the forest, splashing over its banks and nearly covering the large rocks she so often climbed on. The rain had transformed it from its usual weak dribble into a small river. She knew she wasn't supposed to venture beyond it. Yet the woods on the other side grew thicker and wilder. If the perfect photograph existed out here, she knew she'd find it across the creek.

She had hoped for the spiderweb Mama had spoken of or, barring that, a deer or hawk even. Not this forgotten church. Yet here she stood, a twenty-minute walk past the creek, standing before something she'd just moments ago didn't know existed.

Mama would be so proud of the discovery. When she was better, Sadie vowed to escort her here to see it in person. But for now, a photograph would do.

She raised the camera. Through the viewfinder, she framed as much of the church as she could. There was no way to could get the entire steeple in the shot, but she stepped back far enough to at least include its base. With a press of her finger, the camera clicked and whirred.

A twig snapped to her right.

She lowered the camera, letting the photograph it produced float to the ground like an autumn leaf. Barren trees crowded together around her, their bark slick with rain. She waited, hoping to see a deer.

Nothing revealed itself. She was alone.

Sadie picked up the photograph. It was as gray as the sky, as she waited for it to develop. She shook it like she'd seen her father do, but it didn't seem to hurry the process along at all. While she waited, she stepped closer to the church, hoping she might be able to see through the clouded windows.

There was a gap in the fence, the width of three adults. She guessed that's where the gate had been, though there was no sign of it now.

As she passed through, thunder boomed overhead. The sky opened and rain fell in thick, cold sheets. This was what she got for wandering so far from home.

She pulled the hood of her jacket up and hurried to the doorway, huddling beneath the eaves. Fat drops fell from the corners, but she was shielded from the worst of it. She hoped it wouldn't last long.

Sadie slid the camera and her new photograph into the Polaroid's case, snapping it closed before shoving it into her backpack to keep dry. Hands in her jacket pockets, she leaned against the doors and waited. The sky grew darker and she found herself wondering how long she'd been out here. She didn't think it was close to supper time yet, but with the rain it was so hard to tell.

She wished she had a better way to tell what time it was, but she'd traded her Unikitty watch to Casey last week. Things had been tight money-wise since Mama had gotten worse and Casey's paid-in-full lunch card would feed Sadie the rest of the year. Sadie had gotten the better end of that deal, though she didn't think the girl cared. Casey usually gave her lunches away to friends. Sadie sometimes wondered if she had one of the eating disorders they'd talked about in health class.

The wind shifted and cold rain blew into her eyes. She shivered and turned toward the door. The rain pelted her back like a thousand tiny pebbles. Her skin was ice cold and her teeth chattered. She tried the handle to the church, knowing it would be locked and she'd be trapped here in the rain.

"I done told you a hundred times not to cross that creek," Daddy would say when she finally got home. She would get sick and then he would have to care for her, too. She didn't want to do that to him.

The door clicked and creaked open.

Surprised, she hurried inside, the wind catching the door and banging it against the wall. Rain blew in behind her to form a puddle on the floor. Sadie fought the entrance closed again.

It was darker in here than she'd thought it would be. The dirty windows blocked much of the gray outside. What little light leaked through illuminated a dozen or so pews. Old leaves and dried brush littered the floor. Dirt and dust piled inside the windowsills. Plants had burst through the floorboards here and there, most having died and gone brown before they could grow much higher.

Rain beat against the walls and windows, tapped against the roof, but it all had a muted quality. It was as though the outside world had retreated miles away from the church. Even the air inside was strange. It was thick and stale and carried the earthy scent of mildew.

She didn't feel right being here. She felt like she had burst in and interrupted a service. Could something be living here? Raccoons or possums, maybe?

Some drifter, she thought, and that made her shiver more than the rain had.

When her eyes adjusted to the weak light, she stepped carefully around the room, hoping to spot anything that might be making a home here before it spotted her. The place was empty. Not only were there no animals, there were no signs of any. No droppings, no nests, no remains of small rodents or birds that had been eaten.

"Y'all don't know what you're missing out on," she said and instantly regretted it. The sound carried strangely in here and the silence that she had broken rushed back like a physical thing. It made her feel as though someone was about to respond.

As she neared the back of the church, her eyes were drawn to the altar. It was a long table that stood to Sadie's chest. Unlike First Methodist, where the altar sat on a stage, the floor here remained flat. A large and tangled bush had grown around it in stark contrast to the failed attempts at growth dotting the rest of the room. Small branches and vines cradled the altar itself, the bush growing around its sides and forming a rear-wall. Most of it had gone brown as well, and dry leaves dotted the altar and floor, but splashes of green somehow still existed within. It refused to die.

She stepped closer to see what had captured her attention to begin with. She had assumed that what looked like a display on the altar had merely been brush and was surprised to find photographs.

Framed photos, at least twenty, were positioned atop the altar as though it were a fireplace mantle. She grabbed one of the larger ones, a black and white depicting a man in a dark suit. He was thin, almost skeletal, with sharp cheeks and sunken eyes. His hair was slicked back, and a moustache lined his upper lip. Something about his suit and hair reminded Sadie of photographs in her history book. She guessed it to be a hundred years old. Maybe more.

She replaced the photograph, careful to stand it behind the remains of the candle just as she had found it. Each frame owned a candle, she realized. Burned out and covered in dust, rivers of hardened wax ran from the base of each to form stalactites on the edge of the altar. Puddles of wax had dried in a mess on the floor beneath it.

Another picture had the faded color of something from the 1970s, like the photographs of Daddy as a baby. In fact, this one was of a child as well. A girl much younger than Sadie smiled in a blue dress, her blond hair done up in curls and a ribbon.

Each was of a single person and none looked recent. There were photographs of children and adults, of teenagers and the elderly. She guessed the altar had been used for prayer. Didn't the Catholics light candles for their loved ones in need? She thought she'd read that somewhere. It made sense, too, since more than a few of the people framed atop the altar had the look of illness about them. They reminded her of Mama.

Sadie shrugged out of her backpack and removed the camera from its case. She snapped the flash into place and took a photograph of the altar. Returning it to the case to await exposure alongside the other one, she remembered the picture she'd shoved into her pocket earlier.

A crease ran through the center of the now developed Polaroid. Mama looked so pretty inside its white borders, a giant smile on her face and hand raised in mock-protest.

An idea came to Sadie. She adjusted the photographs on the altar until she found a place for Mama. She wished it wasn't the only picture without a frame, but the decades old look of the Polaroid made it at least seem as though it had always been here.

She slid a dusty white candle over from a picture of a soldier in dress blues. The candle was still three inches tall and she was certain it had some life left in it. She didn't see the harm in repurposing it. The photograph looked so old that she figured whatever prayer had been attached to it had already been used.

A lighter sat wedged in her backpack, a remnant from the week last fall she had tried smoking with the Pritchett girls. The rough taste of the cigarettes had been almost as bad as how light-headed they made her. She had given it up, but the lighter had stayed.

She was thankful for it now as she lit the candle. The top flared to life as the dust there caught fire. Within a few seconds it had settled and only the wick burned, flickering and dancing in the empty room.

Something like a sigh passed behind her.

She turned, expecting to see the door open and some adult chastising her for going places she shouldn't. But she was alone.

A trick of the wind outside, no doubt.

Sadie looped her fingers together, lowered her head, and prayed.

"Our Father who art in Heaven, hollow be thy name." She didn't think she got that exactly right, but continued anyway. "I know Mama is getting better even if no one else does. Daddy tells me she's still a long way off and some of the kids at school, they ask if she's dying. Mrs. Rafferty at the corner store told me her husband had to go on Morphine when he got like Mama and that he was dead in a week. Ain't that a cruel thing to tell somebody? Mr. Rafferty was an old man, anyway. Mama's still got plenty of years left in her. I just ask that you help speed up her recovery, that's all. Her birthday's coming up next month and if she could be back on her feet by then, she'd be so happy. So, please, help Mama get better. Amen."

Sadie looked up. The orange glow of the candle cast strange shadows on her mother's face. The sight unnerved her, though she wasn't sure why.

She noticed then how quiet it had grown. The rain had stopped at some point while she prayed. She should hurry home and show Mama what she found.

She closed the doors behind her, leaving the candle to burn into the night.

Forty minutes later, as she approached the house, she saw the ambulance parked in the driveway and forgot all about her photographs.

The funeral was on a Sunday. Sadie refused to join Daddy and Nicky as they approached the coffin. She didn't want to see Mama like that, cold and lifeless. She wanted to remember the vibrant woman with a smile always at the ready. Whatever was in that box, it wasn't her mother.

Daddy hadn't pressed the issue. It had been hard enough on him as it was. Sadie felt guilty for not standing beside him as he looked at Mama, his eyes hollow. He almost dropped Nicky when lifting the boy to see his mother. Nicky simply stared in silence, too young to understand what was happening.

Sadie had been hugged by a hundred people and, for the life of her, couldn't remember a single one. Cousins and neighbors had filled their yard with fold-up tables when they got home, casserole dishes and pie tins steaming atop them. She hadn't waited for anyone else to arrive and instead went straight upstairs to her room and locked the door. Every few minutes someone would knock or whisper some platitude through the wood, but she ignored them.

She lay on her bed, hot tears streaking her face, and stared at one of the first Polaroids she'd taken with her camera. It showed Mama, healthier then, her red hair still thick and the wheelchair yet to make an appearance. She posed in the kitchen, a green and red apron draped over her, batter covered spoon in hand as she smiled.

A twinge of regret hit Sadie for the photograph she left at the ancient church. God had ignored her that day, after all, and she did not like the thought of having abandoned any trace of her mother.

It hit her that Mama never had the chance to see the photographs of the church. She never even got to hear about the discovery. It seemed such an unimportant thing now. Sadie hadn't mentioned it to anyone, hadn't even thought about it since Mama died. She hadn't so much as glanced at the photographs she had taken that day. Were they still in the camera case?

She sat up, wiping her eyes with the back of her hand, and looked around the room. Where had she left the camera?

Another knock at the door distracted her.

"Sadie?" Daddy called through the door. "Open up, would

you?"

Something in her father's voice made her do so. He stepped inside and closed the door behind him. He had always been a large and imposing man, but he looked so small since Mama passed. The exhaustion seemed to have eaten away at him. Even his posture had collapsed in on itself.

"You coming out?" he asked. "Everybody's asking about you."

Sadie folded her arms. She wasn't in the mood to be comforted. "How much longer they all gonna be here?"

"A couple more hours, I reckon." He pulled his daughter into an embrace and kissed the top of her head. "But if you don't feel like being around anybody, you don't have to. I just wanted to check. If nothing else, you should get some of Imogene's sweet potato casserole."

"I think I'll just take a nap. Can you put some casserole in a Tupperware for me?"

He smiled, his red-rimmed eyes moist. "You got it."

When he was gone, she locked her door again. She resumed the search for the camera case, eventually finding it inside of her backpack.

Someone laughed in the hallway outside her door. She wasn't sure why, but it made her angry. She didn't want to be here right now. Even the locked door couldn't provide her with the solitude she craved.

Flipping open the leather case, she removed the two photographs. The one of the altar looked washed out and blurry, as though she'd moved the camera right as the flash had fired. She had hoped to get a good shot of it and was disappointed that she had wasted the film.

The exterior shot, however, was clean and crisp. The church's details seemed carved into the Polaroid. She could easily make out the rain trickling down the fogged-over windows, the subtle lines between the wooden slats that made up the walls, and the doors...

She sat up straighter and held the photograph to her face. It didn't make any sense. The doors had been closed when she approached the church. They had been closed when the rain broke and she huddled beneath the eaves. They had been closed until she opened them.

Yet, in the Polaroid, the left door was open at least a foot.

That wasn't the strangest part. As she examined it closely, she realized that what she had first mistaken for a trick of the light was something else entirely. Though too far from the camera to capture anything other than a blur, and too shadowed to highlight any features, the shape was unmistakable and made her stomach drop.

A face was tucked between the open door and the wall, staring out at her.

Everyone had left by sundown and Sadie microwaved plates of leftovers for Daddy and Nicky. She made a plate for herself, too, but didn't feel much like eating. She picked at lukewarm macaroni and cheese while contemplating the Polaroid. She had heard strange noises that day, but had been certain she'd been alone. Now she wondered if there had been someone at the church, someone who quickly peeked out the door before vanishing through a back exit.

She didn't have any answers and couldn't in good conscience burden her father with the mystery, not with everything he was going through, and so gave up for the time being. She made sure her little brother finished his supper so she could get him ready for bed as Daddy stood silent at the kitchen counter, shovelling his meal down in large, quick bites.

Nicky brushed his teeth and put on his pyjamas with little

fuss, a rare occurrence in their household. When Sadie asked if he wanted her to read him a story, he requested flipping through photographs on Mama's outdated Android tablet instead. He cuddled up against Sadie and sucked on one finger as they did so, the light from the screen illuminating his face in the dark bedroom. She kept stealing glances of him, wondering how much he understood, but his tiny face didn't betray whatever thoughts he might be having. His wide eyes (as blue as Mama's, she thought) remained fixed on the screen.

"Sissy?"

"Yes, Nicky?"

"Where the one we on the choo-choo?"

"The choo-choo? When were we on a choo-choo?"

"The choo-choo," he said, a slight whine in his voice. He did not like it when he felt as though she didn't understand him.

She wracked her brain, trying to think of what he could mean.

"The choo-choo," he repeated, the whine more prevalent.

"Wait." She swiped through the album, looking for the photographs from Christmas.

She finally found the one she hoped for. They had driven all the way to Knoxville to shop at the mall there and were surprised to find a carousel dominating the center of the food court. They'd found a seat decorated to look like a Christmas train. Nicky and Mama had ridden it three times in a row. In the photograph, Mama hugged Nicky tight; the two of them caught mid-laughter as they went around and round. They both looked so happy.

Sadie's breath hitched at the sight.

"Sissy?"

"Yes, Nicky?"

"When Mama come back?"

The tears came hard then. Sadie squeezed her brother tight, kissing the top of his head over and over as she wept.

"Too tight," he finally said, and she released him.

It didn't take long for him to fall asleep. Once he had, Sadie plugged in his Dusty Crophopper nightlight and crept from the room, gently closing the door behind her.

The house was dark. Daddy must have gone to bed early as well. She might as well get ready for bed, too.

While washing her face, she heard a noise from downstairs.

The sound was faint, but reminded her of the Polaroid camera. The click-whir-hum of the camera snapping a picture and then sliding the photograph out was distinctive. Had Nicky crawled out of bed and gotten into her camera case? It wouldn't be the first time he'd done something of the sort.

Face covered with soap and eyes closed, she grasped for the faucet's knobs and turned the water off to listen.

The wind whistled outside, and a tree scratched against the siding every now and then. It was otherwise silent.

She quickly rinsed her face and towelled off. Crossing the hall, she eased her brother's door open. There he was, stuffed cat hugged to his chest, fast asleep. She closed the door.

Shuffling at the bottom of the stairs.

"Daddy?" she called.

The shuffling stopped.

Without thinking, she took a step down the dark staircase. There were two light switches for the overhead light, one a few feet behind her, the other at the bottom of the stairs. She knew she should climb back into the hall and flip that switch on, but the feeling that she had caught someone was strong. The air was alive and expectant. It made her want to sneak farther down the stairs and peek before flipping the light on. What could Daddy be doing down there in the dark, anyway?

She took another step, the wooden stair creaking beneath her weight. She cringed at the sound.

Below her, the living room was black, faint moonlight trickling in to highlight the edges of shadowed furniture. She crouched and leaned forward, gripping the rail on her left tight as she peered down into the dark room. She couldn't make out anything and was about to call down and ask why Daddy didn't turn the lights on.

Then she saw it.

A hand.

It draped over the rail toward the bottom. Slender, feminine, the fingers long and thin, skin pale, it rested on the iron railing from inside the living room, its owner standing there in the dark.

Sadie's breath caught in her throat. She wanted to move, but couldn't. Couldn't make herself step backwards. Couldn't rush down the stairs and flick on the light. She couldn't even yell for Daddy. She could only stand there, skin going cold, as she stared at the hand.

It didn't move, simply stayed there on the rail. Even as her eyes adjusted to the dark, she couldn't make out anything else. The wrist vanished into blackness and whoever was at the other end of the arm did not move or make any sound. Sadie knew they watched her from their place in the living room, that they craned their neck up to see who crouched near the top of the stairs.

Finally, the fingers curled around the rail, veins standing tall as whoever hid there gripped the iron. Gripped it like they were preparing to climb the stairs.

Sadie screamed and ran down the hall, not bothering to turn on the light, crashing through Daddy's door to find him sitting up in bed, the television on. She threw herself into his arms.

Daddy searched the entire house with a pistol in hand and checked every lock. He found no sign of anyone, nor of any locks having been tampered with.

Somehow Nicky slept through the entire thing, which made Sadie feel even sillier.

"It's been a tough time," Daddy said as he returned the pistol to his gun safe. "For all of us."

"Can I sleep with you tonight?"

He sighed and, for a moment, she thought he'd tell her she was too old for that. "Of course," he said. "Let's get your brother, too."

Daddy managed to carry Nicky in without waking him. The three of them curled up together in the queen-size bed where her mother once slept.

The rain returned the following afternoon. Mama's cousin, Maddie, had a boy around Nicky's age and offered to watch him for the day. Daddy thought it would be good for him and so dropped Nicky off. After that, he told Sadie he had some errands to run and not to leave the house. She suspected those errands included downing whiskey by himself in the corner of a bar somewhere, but who was she to judge? She had no idea what it was like to drink and her father never did so at home. Maybe it would help him.

Sadie had the house to herself. Even if Daddy hadn't told her not to, she couldn't imagine going outside in this weather. Rain drummed against the roof and thunder shook the windows. The afternoon sun that should have bathed the house had been devoured by storm clouds. Dark swathes of shadow covered the walls, furniture and floors.

The urge to go through Mama's closet took her. There wasn't anything in particular she looked for, but she found the cool fabric of her mother's clothes comforting. Every now and then, she'd hold a dress up against herself and look in the mirror. She could almost hear her mother in the doorway asking Sadie what she thought she was doing, mock indignation in her voice.

A thud sounded from downstairs and Sadie dropped the dress she held. It crumpled on the floor and she stepped around it, pausing at the entrance to the hall to listen.

The rain and wind sounded louder now, as though it were here in the house with her. There were no other sounds, and she was certain all the doors were locked. She had checked them herself after Daddy and Nicky left.

Wishing she'd known the combination to the gun safe, Sadie crept to the staircase. She expected to see the hand on the rail again, but even in the dull gray light of the storm, she could see the living room clearly. No one was there.

Taking a deep breath, she made her way down the stairs.

Their white curtains, stitched together from the thinnest linen, danced in a cold wind that rushed through an open window. It carried fat drops of rain inside to slap against the floor. Broken glass sparkled on the rug from the picture that had blown over. It was a photograph of her parents on their wedding day; the frame now cracked and broken. She replaced it on the table.

Why hadn't she noticed a window was open earlier?

She flicked the overhead light switch. Nothing happened. She tried again, to no avail. Had the power gone out? The light on the staircase still burned. A fuse must have blown. She'd tell Daddy when he returned and let him descend into the basement to replace it.

She moved toward the kitchen to test the light there, then stopped. Something had creaked. It was the sharp squeal of wood, like someone leaning back in one of the kitchen chairs.

"Just the wind," she muttered, though it did not calm her nerves.

The white curtains still billowed into the room, stretching across like fingers reaching for a loved one. She stepped over to close the window.

Heavy feet whispered through the carpet behind her.

The wind roared outside, cold rain blowing in to stick her shirt to her back as she turned, heart racing, unsure what she might see.

Legs at the top of the staircase. Bare calves and feet vanishing into the upstairs hallway.

The light on the stairs flickered twice before going out.

Trembling, she stepped around to look up the stairs.

The woman stood in darkness at the top, nude and pale, a shadow across her shoulders and head. No hair marred her skin. Sadie knew, somehow, that it was Mama. Even though the woman faced away from her, Sadie knew.

Her mother continued down the hall.

Crying now, Sadie called for Mama and gripped the stair railing. She hurried to the top in time to see her mother disappear into the bedroom she'd shared with Sadie's father.

Sadie followed, slowly entering the room as though a loud noise could dispel whatever magic had been conjured here.

This room, too, was now dark. Her mother stood in the corner on the far side, the bed between her and Sadie.

"Mama," Sadie said again, no other words coming to her.

The muted sound of the storm outside filled the room.

Thicker clouds must have rolled in then, because that side of the room grew even darker. Mama seemed to melt into the black there. She flailed about, or so it seemed. Sadie could make out nothing but writhing shadows.

One peeled off from the rest and moved across the room. It hunched over, the gnarled and twisted spine pressing out through its flesh threatening to break free and run. Thin arms swam out into the room, knobby knuckled hands reaching with fingers like thin, aged paper wrapping dry twigs. It shuffled forward, an awkward dance of disjointed legs never intended to move. A creaking moan leaked from somewhere above its mangled neck.

Why am I here?

It wasn't speech so much as tepid water trickling into Sadie's ears.

She turned and ran.

Her mind didn't have time to process her fear as she scrambled down the steps. Ancient nerves in her spine prodded her on, evolution's patchwork of early warning systems forcing her away from danger before she even knew what she ran from.

In the front yard, she sat under a willow tree, knees hugged to her cold chest, and watched the open front door until Daddy came home. Even as he carried her inside and asked what was wrong, all she could think about was Mama disappearing into the dark and the thing that emerged when she did. It shuffled toward her. It reached for her. And its face...

Its face was the same that peeked through the church doors in her Polaroid.

Later, sitting in front of the fireplace with a blanket wrapped around her and a mug of hot chocolate steaming in her hands, her father told her the story.

"Ain't nobody lived on the Rutledge Farm in ages," he said. "But back when my Daddy was a boy, there was stories going around about them. That was before they sold most of their land to Big South Fork. Since it became part of the National Park, I don't guess anyone much talks about it.

"Back then, though, they still had a farmhouse and some other buildings up on the property. They tore them all down back when I was about your age, but some had been up since God knows when. Not sure who owned it before them, but it was supposed to be one of the first farms ever around here.

"Anyway, Daddy said people stayed away from the Rutledge Farm back then. This would have been the late forties, I reckon. He said everybody had one ghost story or another about the property."

"Ghost story?" Sadie interrupted.

"Yeah. Silly stuff, mostly. Lights in the woods at night, people heard talking when there weren't no one there, that sort of thing. Mostly, though, people stayed away because of the Rutledge Family themselves.

"Old Man Rutledge used to lay a 30-aught-6 across his lap and drive his tractor around their fields, shooting at nothing in particular. People thought he was either crazy or a drunk, maybe both, but it was like he patrolled the land expecting trespassers.

"His boys weren't much better. His oldest, Nate was his name, he killed another boy in shop class. Beat him to death with a hammer for smarting off. They sent him up to Brushy Mountain. He got let go on parole in the sixties and came back to the farm. Rumor was, he lived out in the woods and refused to go anywhere near the farmhouse. A few years later, his older brother Samuel hung himself in the barn there. They said Samuel was one mean S-O-B, too."

"Did Grampa ever see any of the ghost lights or anything?"

"I don't know what he saw. He said his dog got away from him once when he was little. Said it went racing across the creek. He chased it into the woods there and... Well. He did see something."

"What?" Sadie wondered if her palms sweat from the heat of the fire or the story her father told.

"He never would tell. He'd only say it scared the hell out of him. He never crossed that creek again and, when we were kids, he never let us do it, neither. I guess that's one of the reasons I made that rule with you, too. Kind of tradition, I suppose. Course, kids being kids, we broke the rule once ourselves."

"You did? Did you see anything?"

"I didn't see nothing, no. But there was this... It was like we was being watched the whole time, like someone was following us around. Every time one of us would think we heard a noise behind us, or felt someone off to our side, we'd spin around, just itching to catch them. But we never did.

"I never went back there again. Not because it was so weird, though it was. But there's just no reason to. Nothing but woods on that land, and you ain't even allowed to hunt on it, so what's the point?"

Sadie sipped her hot cocoa. Nicky murmured to himself in the corner as he drove Hot Wheels around on the carpet and, for a moment, she wished she were that young again.

"Now, this picture here." Daddy held the Polaroid of the church up. "You swear this is the same person who was here in the house?"

"I think so, Daddy, yeah."

He nodded slowly and examined it again. "And this church. How far out is it?"

"Not close, but not too far. Maybe a twenty-minute walk."

He was quiet for a long while, his eyes narrowed into what she recognized as his thinking face. Then he slid the photograph into his pocket. "I tell you what I think happens out there. What's probably happened for fifty years or more. I think drifters hole up in that church."

"It wasn't a drifter."

"They get off the interstate," he said, ignoring her, "right there at that exit with the big Pilot station. Then they wander around looking for work as farmhands or what have you. Problem is, most of that work dried up a long time ago. Some hitchhike back out of here. Others wander around some more and try to make a go of things.

"This fella in the church, he probably followed you back here when he saw you in the woods that day. Probably hoped to steal something. Or worse. I want you to stay in the house the next couple of days when you're not at school. It's too late today, but tomorrow I'll get some of the boys together after work and we'll go out there and have ourselves a look."

"What about Mama?"

He stared at her and she could see the disbelief on his face.

"Sadie..." he started.

"I saw her, Daddy. She was here."

"That's not... It just ain't possible."

"It's that church," she said, knowing it was somehow true. "I put that picture there and lit a candle, just like all the others, and she came back."

"What happened was that this drifter scared you near senseless and you thought you saw something. Christ, Sadie, we just put your Mama in the ground yesterday."

"She was in the house, Daddy."

"Stop it." His face had gone red and she knew she made him

angry. Still, she couldn't pretend like none of it had ever happened.

"I saw her," she said, "plain as day, just like I see you now."

"I said stop it."

"She climbed the stairs and went into your room. She was here."

"Then why ain't I seen her, huh?" Tears broke free to stream down her father's face. He shook and she realized that what she had mistaken for anger was something else. "If your Mama's here, why can't I get to see her? Huh?"

He made a trembling fist and brought it up to his face. He closed his eyes, pressed a knuckle against his forehead, and sucked a sharp breath.

Sadie ran to him, threw her arms around his waist and buried her head in his chest.

"I miss her so much." His voice was weak.

She held him tight, something breaking inside of her at the sight. He had always been the rock for the entire household, had always brought calm and strength whenever they needed it, and to see what Mama's loss and Sadie's talk of ghosts did to him made her cry, too.

She made the decision right there not to tell him about any of this again.

Mama returned that night. Daddy slept on the sofa, pistol under his pillow and a baseball bat on the floor beside him. He had triple-checked every lock, but, having convinced himself that the intruder was a man, he was not going to take any chances someone might slip by him.

Sadie read *The Big Blue Truck* to Nicky until he dozed off and then crawled into her own bed. She had considered sleeping with her brother, not wanting him to be alone. But it occurred to her that, whatever walked through this house, it had come for her. She had been the one to place the photograph on the altar, after all. She had been the one to light the candle. What she summoned was hers alone. Best to keep that away from Nicky.

She couldn't sleep and instead lay in the dark, listening for strange noises and running the situation through her mind over and over. If there were ghost stories about that land, they certainly made sense. The altar could not be a simple place for prayer, not after what she'd seen. Had all the people pictured atop it died only to be summoned back here? Where they still out there wandering the woods? And, when they came, did they always bring with them the thing she saw?

She thought of Old Man Rutledge patrolling the land on his tractor, gun at the ready for trespassers he was sure would come.

Footsteps sounded on the stairs. They were soft and moved slowly. She turned to her closed door, certain they weren't her father's. He walked with heavy feet and always thudded up the steps.

The sound moved to the hallway, shuffling past her door.

The hall went silent.

Then the shuffling returned, this time stopping outside her bedroom.

She reached for the lamp on her bedside table and tugged the pull-string. It clicked, but did not emit any light. She tried again. Nothing.

She stared at the doorknob, certain it would jiggle or turn.

The silence stretched on and it was unbearable.

Then the shuffling sounded from behind her.

She scrambled off the bed, a scream caught in her throat, and pressed against the bedroom door. A darkness blossomed in the corner, growing, unfolding. She could find no detail there, but did not want to wait and see what would emerge.

Afraid to make a sound, she opened the door and slipped through, closing it behind her. The hallway was empty and she almost laughed in relief.

She stepped over to the staircase only to catch sight of Mama at the bottom, passing from the landing and into the dark of the living room.

Sadie waited, certain she would hear her father wake below, but his gentle snoring continued without interruption.

She curled up on the floor in Nicky's room the rest of the night. She didn't sleep, but instead kept her eyes on the soft orange glow of his nightlight to be certain it never went out.

In the morning, she would bring an end to this. She had no other choice.

Exhausted, she was tempted to stay home the next day. Daddy had told her she didn't have to go back to school until she was ready. But she took a shower all the same and climbed down the stairs to eat bacon and eggs before walking to the bus stop.

When she neared the stop, three other kids stood with their hands in their pockets, breath misting in the cold morning air as they laughed at some joke. Before they could see her, she darted across Mr. Lawson's yard and into the woods.

The forest was damp, and an early morning mist shrouded the view around her. It took some backtracking to reach the creek, but, once she did, she wondered if this was the best course of action. Now that she knew what that church did and what likely roamed the woods here, the idea of crossing the boundary frightened her.

The responsibility was hers, though. She had started all of

this. Had Mama's death even come because Sadie had lit that candle? The timing of it seemed more than a coincidence.

She wiped the tears away and refused to think about it. Not now, at least. Not until her mistake had been undone.

"God," she said. "Help me let Mama rest."

Sadie took a deep breath and crossed the creek.

The woods here were quiet, but she no longer felt alone. Daddy's story must have gotten to her because she felt eyes on her; felt like someone stalked behind her. No matter how quickly she turned, she caught sight of no one. The mist didn't help. Anything more than thirty feet from her had become hazy gray shadow.

As she hiked deeper, the feelings grew stronger. Twice she thought she heard voices off to the side. Yet when she stopped to listen, silence.

The church seemed to materialize in the mist before her. She stopped at the kudzu covered fence, hands on the straps of her backpack, and waited. For what, she didn't know, but the air was alive with the dread sense something would occur soon.

Rustling in the brush off to her right. She turned in time to see an impossibly tall figure, gaunt with gray skin, take two large, loping strides before vanishing into the mist-shrouded woods.

A part of her wanted to sprint back through the forest and across the creek, but she was afraid that if she did, the things wandering around out here would give chase. And if she made it home, Mama would come again. When she did, the others wouldn't be far behind.

Sadie passed through the gap in the fence and entered the church.

From inside, it would be easy to think night had fallen. The early morning light did not fight very hard to push through the clouded windows. As a result, the room was painted in thick shadow. The faint light passing through the open door did little to dispel any of it.

Shrugging her backpack off, Sadie dug around inside for the lighter. She thumbed the flint, and nothing happened. She tried again and still nothing. Panic took her as she continued, trying frantically to get so much as a spark.

On her sixth try, the lighter flared to life and she released the breath she hadn't realized she'd been holding. Its dim orange glow carved a short path into the darkness. Sadie stepped slowly, examining the black on either side of her, afraid of what might be waiting there.

When she reached the altar, she was surprised to find a tiny ember still glowing on her mother's candle. She held the lighter's flame to it, reigniting the wick. The candle had burned down to almost nothing. She wouldn't have much time.

The flame illuminated the Polaroid of Mama and Sadie hesitated at the sight.

Feet shuffled behind her. She turned to see a slight figure in the doorway. Little more than silhouette, it watched in stillness.

"Mama," Sadie said. "I'm sorry."

The figure didn't move.

Sadie turned and grabbed the Polaroid. She held its corner in the flame of the candle. The plastic curled and blackened, foul smelling smoke drifting from it, before it caught on fire. The flame quickly crawled up its side and burned Sadie's fingers. She tossed it away from her, ashes dusting the air as the burning photograph drifted to the ground.

The figure in the doorway could no longer be seen.

A manic desperation taking hold, Sadie lit each of the remaining candles on the altar. She smashed the frames onto the floor, broken glass dusting the wood, and set each of them on fire. Footsteps sounded around her, a dozen, two dozen, shuffling about in agitation, but she ignored them and continued her work. Soon a pile of melting plastic burned at her feet and the church filled with smoke.

She took a step back and brushed against a dry wooden limb on the bush. It snagged her shirt.

When she turned to free herself, she screamed.

The bush sat several feet away. Yet the knobby, desiccated thing gripping her shirt was the same as had pulled itself from darkness in her parents' bedroom. Its blurry, featureless face the same as the photograph she'd taken of it. She ripped free of its grip and tumbled into the fire, ashes and charred fragments of photographs flying into the air like a macabre confetti.

It came for her, shuffling awkwardly, hands clawing at the air as she scrambled backwards on her hands and feet.

I came for you

Again, the words washed over, less speech than some kind of change in the air pressure. She fought to her feet and hurried around the room, slamming her knee into a pew as she did. She grunted and limped on, the thing shuffling through the dark behind her.

Sadie made it back to the altar, the candles burning brightly atop it. The shadow moved closer, circling around the back of the bush.

You called me here

Gripping the bottom of the altar with both hands, Sadie flipped it over into the bush, the candles tumbling into the growth. Within seconds, the dry plant caught fire.

Her pursuer recoiled from the flame, tumbled backwards into the darkness along the wall.

I am afraid

A twinge of pity passed through Sadie as she sprinted for the open door. She ran through the woods as fast as her legs would carry her.

It wasn't long until she heard them chasing after her.

That night, her father told her that he and some friends went out into the woods, just as he'd promised. They found the smoldering remains of the church and assumed one of the mythical drifters he spoke of had been responsible for the fire. If not for the weather, the whole forest could have gone up. He informed the Sheriff, though nothing ever came of it.

Weeks went by and they adjusted to a life without Mama. Sadie missed her every day, but the tears did not come so often. She even found herself laughing now and then.

Then, one night in early May, she couldn't sleep. Summer's humidity had come early and she lay atop her sheets, window open, annoyed at the sweat gathering behind her knees. She clicked her ceiling fan to its highest setting and thought she might read. When she stepped over to the bookshelf, she saw the case for her Polaroid sitting alongside a teddy bear and a trophy she'd received for softball in fourth grade.

She hadn't touched the camera since everything happened and took it down to examine. As she opened the case, a single photograph slid out and fluttered to the ground.

The memory came back to her then. She had heard the noise of her camera snapping a picture the first night Mama had returned. Who had used the camera? And what had they taken a photograph of?

She thought of the shadow that spoke to her and shivered.

You called me here, it had said, if such a thing could even be considered speech.

I am afraid

Hands trembling, afraid of what she might see, she bent to retrieve the picture.

As she did, something shuffled on the carpet behind her.

6.

The first thing I did after reading the next story was to dust off my end of fifth year school group photograph and stare nostalgically at the assembly of young faces frozen in front of the haunted 19th century mansion school house. I was saddened by how little of my interactions with them were a pleasant experience to remember; a few were downright nightmarish to replay in my mind. So, unlike the protagonist in Mr. Little's story, there's absolutely no way I would agree to return to the building where it all took place. I'm sending my school ghosts back to where they belong - inside the gym closet with my unclaimed sweaty socks and the spongy green mat stained with my blood and tears.

THEY SAY YOU SHOULD NEVER GO BACK

by David Little

Laurence was the first one to contact me. He sent on a text that late October morning. It sent my phone into a vibrating frenzy of activity that managed to wake me out of a cocktail induced slumber. I rubbed my eyes for a few seconds and then looked at the screen, to see the dark letters of Laurence's text cut through the white background.

THEY'RE TEARING DOWN OUR HIGH SCHOOL!!!

My thumbs stumbled over the touch screen keyboard.

ABOUT TIME! WHEN?

It was shortly after four in the morning, which immediately made me wonder what the hell Laurence was doing up at this time?

Phone in hand, I threw back the duvet cover and slid out of bed before half walking, half staggering towards the kettle.

As I made myself a coffee, I kept an eye on the screen for Laurence's response.

Frustratingly, it wasn't forthcoming, so I took my mug over to the kitchen table that doubled as my work from home desk. A dark blue business card was next to my laptop. It had been given to me by a counsellor that I had been seeing, and was for a university behavioural science group who were willing to pay people to take part in their research project.

I checked my e-mails. There was one from my old school friend, Charlene Wilson, entitled: THEY'RE PULLING IT DOWN!!!

The majority of the text was cut and pasted from some website as it was littered with official terminology, and what I would describe as 'council speak' - if such a thing existed. The more salient points were that it had closed down six years ago, as a larger school had been built to reflect a restructuring of the catchment area. Due to a downturn in the economy, the council had been unable to sell the land as previously planned, but now they had agreed on a reduced fee with a buyer who was set to build a housing estate there. The brief biography of the building ended by announcing that the demolition was to take place the following week. This was then followed by a message from Charlene:

I'M GOING TO GO SEE IT. YOU SHOULD COME.

This initially surprised me, given that Charlene felt the exact same way as I did about the school. We truly hated almost every minute of our time there.

As I took a final swig of my coffee to drain the cup, my eyes drifted downwards across what seemed like a vast space in the screen to see some other words.

I'M GOING TO BURN IT TO THE GROUND.

Reading those words I really didn't know what to think. She

couldn't be serious, could she?

Laurence finally texted back.

CHARLENE WANTS TO BURN THE PLACE DOWN. YOU IN?

At that moment I decided that I needed to be at her side.

Travelling on a train later that afternoon, I was all alone in the carriage, except for a middle-aged man in a crisply pressed, pin-striped suit, who sat facing me for the entire three hour journey.

The man did nothing except read the pile of newspapers on the seat beside him from cover to cover. It was sort of fascinating to watch; how he would methodically scan each page in turn from top to bottom, his head moving from left to right, then down a bit, and then left to right once more until the page was finished. Then his head would move to the opposite page where he repeated this back and forth until he finished. By the time we arrived at my destination, I'm sure he must have read each newspaper at least three times.

I was a little surprised to find Charlene waiting for me outside the train station. She sat cross-legged on top of the bonnet of a red mini cooper. Her hair, which when young switched between brunette, copper and blonde almost with the seasons, now had streaks of grey in it.

The drive to her house was subdued. At no time did either of us mention the email or the impending arson. Eventually, we pulled up outside a semi-detached house in a cul-de-sac. Beyond the driveway, atop the stairs that led to the front door, stood Laurence and another of our old school friends, Val.

"They got here quickly," I said.

"They know not to defy my instruction," she joked, opening the car door. "As, of course, do you."

We hugged and chatted briefly, but it was all superficial. I could tell by the way they were acting; occasionally quiet and distant; always looking around to see who might be listening in; peppering any conversation we did have with nervous laughter. I consoled myself with the thought that, once we were done with this task, we would be able to settle down for a night of drinking, eating and making up for lost time.

It was at exactly 10 p.m. when Charlene gave us the nod to get out of the car. It was a tight fit having the four of us in there, together with assorted backpacks and other layers of clothing, not to mention the four cans of petrol that sat between our legs.

We each took a backpack out of the car and opened them, slipping the petrol cans inside before zipping them closed again. Then we pulled the backpacks up to our backs and slipped the straps over our shoulders. I was a little surprised that the weight wasn't as bad as I had thought it would be; but then again, I had never put a can of petrol on my back before, so what did I know.

As we began our slow walk down the hill towards the school grounds, it struck me that none of us had said anything for quite some time. No quips from Laurence trying to make light of the situation; no snide remarks from Val looking to knock us down a peg or two. Charlene hadn't attempted to rally us on, or to give us orders. She just pointed or shook her head to let us know what the next step was.

At the bottom of the hill, we came to a wire mesh fence which must have been about ten feet high. I looked to Charlene and noticed that she had switched on her torch. She shone the light over to a spot on the ground a few metres away. It revealed a large, roughly cut hole in the fence. Val crouched down onto her hands & knees and crawled through the space. She stood up inside the perimeter and nodded towards Laurence, who then did the same. I followed him, and Charlene brought up the rear.

As we got closer, something about the place made me feel uneasy. The buildings that linked together to make up the school campus were in almost total darkness; which meant that just the outline was visible; illuminated from behind by the moon that hung in the middle of the cloudless sky. The school loomed over us like some sort of oppressive force. Seeing it like that made it seem as though it had a weight to it that it never seemed to have when I was a pupil; not physical weight, psychological weight. I wasn't the only one who felt it, because as we reached the bank of steps that led to the front door, I felt Charlene's hand slip into mine and squeeze.

The stairs were illuminated by the light that shone within the reception area, behind the large glass front doors. We hadn't been expecting any lights to be on, and at that moment I silently wondered whether security was more on the ball than Charlene had expected.

After waiting for a minute or two, and seeing no movement from within, we made our way slowly up the stairs.

There was no need to pick the lock or break the glass in the doors, as they were unlocked. We discovered this when Charlene tried to pull one open and it gave easily. The door swung out wide and Charlene stepped back, gesturing for us to walk inside.

The reception hall hadn't changed a bit. Immediately in front of us was the large, horseshoe-shaped desk which stretched from one side of the wall around to the other. A single computer monitor sat atop the desk, power cable hanging down from the back and swinging gently in the draft we had caused on entry. Behind the desk was the school crest; a strange combination of a stag rearing up on its hind legs with an arrow stuck in its front-right fetlock. Our history teacher, Mr. McCormick had explained it was related to the myth of Achilles, but a few years ago, when I mentioned this to a friend who went to vet school, they dismissed it as rubbish as the fetlock is not equivalent to a human heel. What none of our teachers were ever able to explain was why we had a wounded animal on our school crest. I liked to think it was a metaphor for the pupils who attended.

I glanced up the corridor to the left and saw the entrance to the gymnasium.

Like a lot of children, I hated the gym and thought it was run by sick sadists, hiding behind the guise of Physical Education teachers. I, and so many like me, would end up bloodied & bruised by tennis rackets, hockey sticks and hard leather balls struck by classmates who either loved physical education, or who were desperate to inflict pain first to save themselves being on the receiving end.

I stopped replaying memories as a sound was annoying me. It was a steady, pulsing beep that seemed to be coming from every direction at once.

"What is it?" Val asked, obviously having picked up that something was bothering me.

"Do you hear that beeping?" I asked.

"What beeping?"

"That incessant beeping. Can't you hear it? It's everywhere!"

"I don't hear -" Laurence said, but Charlene cut him off.

"It's the fire detection system. It beeps constantly because the smoke detectors and suppression systems have been disconnected. They had to do it because the demolition would cause the alarms to go off and the gas to be expelled."

"How do you know this stuff?" Laurence asked.

"Plied it out of one of the security guards last night," Charlene replied. "Pretended I was a local journalist for the free paper and made him seem important for a bit. It's how I knew there were no security alarms in place either." She pulled the rucksack off her back and placed it on the ground before unzipping it. "We'd be better splitting up. We can cover a greater area that way."

"Wouldn't it be better to stick together?" Laurence asked.

His eyes moved rapidly back and forth between Charlene and Val, looking for some sign from them that he was right.

Charlene rolled her eyes and he knew that it wasn't going to happen.

"We don't have a lot of time," Val said softly. "Better to hit different areas to maximise the impact. Get the fire to spread throughout the buildings."

"I just thought-"

"Look, if you're scared, you can just piss off out of here," Charlene said. "Otherwise, take out your can of petrol, pick a direction, and get moving!"

Laurence turned to me, his face a mixture of fear and sadness.

I looked him square in the eyes, knowing that if I didn't do something assertive, I would be right behind him out the door. "You take the canteen, and I'll take the gym."

He nodded, reluctantly.

"I'll take the science building," Val said.

"Fine," Charlene said. "I'm going to head up to the second floor. I think the library is still fully stocked; and in any case, the stationery and supplies are all there. Right. Back here in twenty minutes, okay?"

Val and I nodded in agreement as Laurence struggled with the zipper on his backpack.

I walked slowly but purposefully down the corridor towards the gym. All the while, my left hand was trembling as it had been since I entered the building.

I pushed open the large double doors and was immediately hit by a powerful smell of floor polish. It was slightly sweet, but with a musty follow through which was a result of the sweat left by generations of children.

Like the reception area, things in the gym were exactly as I remembered from my time as a pupil there. The two long walls had wooden climbing frames which could easily be pulled out to make even more devilishly hard and nightmare-inducing structures for the children to navigate. Along the floor in front of them sat the long wooden benches which had several uses over the years... from highly uncomfortable seats when we had to sit through hours of mind-numbingly pointless assemblies... to when one would be stretched across the climbing frames to create a narrow and wobbly bridge that we had to crawl across. I remembered vividly how I would often get stuck half-way across and could not move with fear. All the while, the P.E. teacher would chuckle. Bastard.

At the far side of the gym was the raised stage where the choir would stand during said assemblies and other musical numbers; or where amateur dramatic productions were held when The Drama Club got too excited and decided to produce one of their amateur scripts. From a distance, the thick maroon curtains looked to be in quite a good condition. They were drawn closed, though I kept waiting for them to part majestically to reveal some sort of pantomime setup.

Then from out of the corner of my eye, I saw movement. I spun around to see what it was, but there was nothing there other than the pillars of red plastic chairs that were stacked side by side, waiting to be spread out for a morning assembly that'll never happen again. Some of the stacks looked precarious, so I wondered whether a good breeze could cause them to sway and mimic a moving body?

The sound of footsteps slipping and running across polished flooring caused me to jump. I turned around to my left and looked up at the stage; the thick, maroon coloured curtains were moving ever so slightly as if something had run between them.

There was definitely someone else here and I was almost certain it wasn't security. They wouldn't be running away from me. I focused on one of my friends being the culprit. One last attempt to scare me out of my wits before we said a final fiery farewell to our childhood. This calmed me down a little, but I knew that I couldn't write it off as a prank unless I caught which one was behind it.

I climbed onto the stage and headed towards the curtains. When there, I held out my hand and grabbed a fistful of material. It was thick and much coarser than I remembered, but even after all these years, I was sure they were the same curtains that had been there when I was a pupil.

With trepidation, I pulled the curtain forward until it parted and looked behind it. On the other side, there were large patches of pink & blue material which had been sown on years ago to cover damaged parts of the inner lining. I remembered that one of them was there because Lawrence and I had cut it up by accident while pretending to sword fight during gym class. I remember the face of the support teacher who took us for P.E. at the time; as every thrust of the jagged wooden planks we were using tore deeper into the curtains, even as he struggled to pull them free. I allowed myself a smile at the memory.

The sound of a chair scraping across the floor behind me caused me to spin around. When I saw the figure of a woman standing near the back of the gym hall, I felt a chill race up my entire body. While my mind rapidly tried to rationalise the figure, believing it must be Charlene or Val, I quickly realised the futility of it. The woman was dressed in a long white lab coat. Her hair was dark and tied tightly at the back in a ponytail. Cradled in the crook of her left arm there was a large, dark rectangular shape that looked like a book of some sort. But something was wrong, and it took me a few seconds to realise what it was. The woman was no more than twenty feet away from me and yet I could make out no details of her face. She had features, of that I was sure, but they were blurred as if she was moving at speed. Yet she was standing absolutely still; no part of her was moving, not even her head.

A shiver hit the back of my neck and I shook physically, stumbling backwards. As I did so, I felt the curtains behind me part and instinctively my hands shot out either side and tried to grab hold, but they slipped impossibly across the rough surface. I felt the material wrap around me like a boa constrictor, covering my torso and arms, before finally swallowing my head. I felt tears welling up inside me as my brain locked onto the logical outcome that I was going to be smothered to death.

It was, therefore, a surprise when my back and then my head hit solid wood, closely followed by my shoulders and hands as they fell loosely to my side. I opened my eyes to find myself lying on the stage looking up at the ceiling. My focus was on the pelmet that stretched across the top of the stage and which protected the curtains that were now hanging straight and silent. The bottoms of the curtains gently brushed at the soles of my boots. Unless the gym was the same on either side of the curtains, I had seemingly fallen back out where I had come in.

I turned over and placed both hands on the stage floor, before pushing myself up to my knees. As I did so, I looked out towards where I had seen the figure, but she was no longer there. The rest of the gym was as I remembered, except for one thing; the can of petrol was no longer there.

I leapt down from the stage and ran back to the reception area.

There was no one else there; which made sense as they were no doubt following through with their own targets.

I knew that Charlene would be the one least likely to give up and go home, so I headed over to the stairway. I jumped up three steps from the bottom and grabbed hold of the black plastic railing which I used to help propel me further upwards.

At the top, I stopped for a few seconds to take a breath and found that I was suddenly exhausted. The run had taken far more out of me than I had expected, and I felt a swell of pressure shooting up my neck and into my head. The world tilted before my eyes and I dropped to the floor, hitting my head again.

I lay there for a few minutes, hoping it would help to alleviate the pain. I heard that damn beeping again. The slow pulsing was now a much more rapid and urgent announcement.

Behind my head I heard a shuffling; like a wet mop sploshing along the floor as it cleaned. I closed my eyes tightly and a vision hit me; a vision of something with too many arms and legs slapping things that weren't quite palms on top of the floor and pulling its twisted and spasming torso closer and closer to me.

Could I outrun it?

I scrambled to my feet and ran down the hall.

It was much longer than I remembered, with many more doors than it should have had. I lunged towards one, grabbing the handle and pushing down; it didn't budge. Neither did the handle on the next door... or the next door... or the next door.

I recognised the room where I had English class during my sixth year. There was a note taped to the door which read QUIET. EXAM IN PROGRESS and I knew that this was where I would find an escape.

The classroom was exactly as I remembered it. The wooden topped desks attached to tarnished metal legs that bent around and up to support the wooden, low backed seat. The blackboard which seemed to stretch across most of the front wall of the room, with thin vertical spaces either side upon which hung safety notices, class role rotas and a smattering of pupil's drawings. The wall that ran along the side of the corridor had paintings that were hung precariously in place by one small golden thumbtack each. The other large wall was just a procession of windows, but each one seemed to be of a slightly different dimension.

In the far corner, sat the man from the train. He was dressed in a long white lab coat and reading someone's classwork; a thin book covered in flowery wallpaper to help distinguish which was theirs amongst the thirty or so other pupils. Again he read across one page from left to right and down, before moving to the top of the next. Once he finished the jotter, he dropped it in a large pile on the floor to his side and picked up another from an even larger pile that seemed to tower precariously over him.

I looked away for a moment, and when I looked back they weren't jotters any more, they were clipboards - like the ones that detail a patient's medical condition.

"You're late Kevin."

I turned to see Charlene standing behind the teacher's desk. She was also dressed in a long white lab coat, and was holding a clear plastic ruler in her right hand, which she was tapping rhythmically against her thigh; the beat matching the pulsing beep of the alarm.

"I'm sorry miss," I said, my voice sounding higher than usual.

She pointed to the desk at the front of the classroom, and I slowly shuffled over to it.

Charlene came out from behind her desk and walked over to me, her high heels clicking rhythmically on the floor and echoing around the room. She placed a blank sheet of paper in front of me. "This is going to be part of your final grading. So make sure your spelling and punctuation are correct; and, above all, that your handwriting is neat and legible. None of your usual chicken scratch."

"Of course, miss."

"And remember," Charlene said as she walked back around her desk and sat down, "if you need more paper, just let me know."

"Yes, miss."

I closed my eyes (or did I open them?) and started writing my school story; the same story I write every night. And I know I shall end up here again, and the story will never, never end.

7.

A TROUBLESOME HISTORY

by Jim Moon

I do remember it vividly, no matter what anyone else says. Every Sunday, we would go to my grandmother's house for tea. And I do mean every Sunday, without fail. The only exceptions were if we were on holiday, or if Christmas Day should fall upon a Sunday. I think we went almost religiously every week as it was continuing proof for the litany I now guess ran through my father's head. Dad was the youngest of three brothers, and the only one who hadn't taken the opportunity to leave this little town as soon as possible.

My uncles had long moved away and become very successful men. But to me they were less than shadows, merely names mentioned at the dinner table, scribbled names read from occasional scribbled postcards that came around as infrequently as comets. I don't think they ever came to visit, or at least I don't recall ever meeting them in childhood. Hence, I think dad saw himself as the good son. He might not be successful, but he had stayed to do his filial duty, and what's more proved it with every Sunday tea. In many ways, I think I am my father's son - I have stayed to do my duty, here in this rainy little town that few have heard of. I sometimes wonder about getting involved in local history. I have always had the desire to tell this town's story, and mostly put it down to what I suspect is a common feeling for many - that you grew up in a place never mentioned in the news nor history books. But, deep down, wouldn't finding something that could put us on the map mean that my dad hadn't wasted his life in a nothing place? And perhaps, as middle years have started to creep up on me, to prove that I too have not squandered my time in a town of little relevance to the rest of the country, and one that is seemingly even slowly fading from memory.

It was not always this way. Once the town was the beating heart of the region. In medieval times, kings and bishops came to hunt in the forests, and later fortunes were made in timber. With the industrial age came mills that never stopped, and canals carrying our wood far and wide. In more recent history, an early adoption of rail saw pit villages spring up around the town and steam trains carrying Redvale coal to the farthest corners of the Empire. But mills are silent now, the mines closed, and the railway is merely a dead-end spur far from the mainline. When occasional visitors come to the town, they must wonder why such a little town with so few trains passing through has just a grand station.

Anyway, as I said, every Sunday we were herded into dad's little car and the trek across town was made. If I close my eyes, I can conjure up every turn and junction, see the town again as it was back in the early '70s. Even when we moved out of town, although only to an outlying village, the Sabbath tea with grandmother continued, even though it meant a ten mile round trip.

Funnily enough, we didn't live out in the sticks for long, just one long winter in 1974. Travelling into town, we gained a new set of streets and lanes before the usual familiar path began when we reached the town centre. Coming in from the north, we wound our way into town on a little road that leads through Auckland Hill, that once upon a time had been a satellite village of the town. But before we reached the main road that ploughed downhill past the old railway works and the grand old shops that marked the beginning of the town centre, we passed through quiet sleepy streets of houses that had seen better days; once a fashionable end of town.

There was one house that always caught my eye. Indeed,

caught my imagination. For in the midst of suburban semi-detached houses was an old set of black wrought-iron gates in an eroded sandstone wall enclosing dark trees. Beyond the gates and through the whispering branches you could just see an old house, which to my child's eyes looked like a mansion. On those Sunday round trips, I always used to look out for that wall and try to get a glimpse of the lonely house, that even back then struck me as strangely marooned amid the little red brick homes. That winter was long, wet and dark, and often I could see the house through the dripping trees, and it was always a thrill if I caught sight of a lighted window or white smoke rising up into the dark clouds like ghosts going to heaven.

I wondered what it was like inside. Antiques and opulences, like the stately homes I'd seen on the telly. Or was it all dusty candelabras and cobwebs, a playground for the richest spiders in town. And who lived there? Some family with riches we could only dream of; or some old miser, as solitary as Scrooge? And while those long dark Sunday car rides were only a small fraction of my childhood days, those stolen glimpses of Malvern House never left me.

Years went by, and their details need not trouble us here. Suffice to stay, a job at Dad's office awaited when the school bell rang a final time, and so the cycle shuffled on. The apple didn't fall far from the tree in many respects. The only unexpected deviation came by chance as I wandered in the local library one day. I had headed into the reference section and stumbled on a display marked 'The Lost Houses of Wynward'. It was several boards of old paintings, etchings and photos of the grand homes built in yesteryear by the great and the good of the town. Many were gone, long since razed and built over, but some I recognised, houses now stripped of their gardens and grounds, frequently swallowed up by the expanding town and often remodelled or rebuilt and pressed into service as municipal buildings.

However it was a smudgy charcoal sketch that caught my

eye. I recognised it instantly - the heavy iron gates and dark trees. A couple of questions secured me the details of the local history group responsible for the display, and a week later I attended my first meeting.

And so it began, after years of not really being interested that much by anything, late in life I found a passion. Possibly a self serving one, but a passion nonetheless. And what deep subconscious currents stirred me, I genuinely adored exploring the town's history, and indeed being active in preserving it. Of course, I took a special interest in trying to piece together the history of Malvern House. But the subject of my childhood fascination was not to give up its secrets easily. It would take years to gather the outline I will set down here. As any historian will tell you, no story is ever truly complete, and certainly there are still many questions about Malvern House. I hope that preserving my research may at least answer several queries those who next investigate may have.

The basics were relatively simple to ascertain. Malvern House was built in November 1898 on what is now Pevennsie Crescent; just off Warren Road. It was constructed by one Terence Lurgan, an Irish-born carpenter who had established a thriving furniture business, and later made a fortune as a timber merchant. However, despite rising into the upper echelons of society, Lurgan never lost touch with his humble roots. Reportedly he mucked in with the carpentry chores on the new house, and it was claimed he built much of the original fittings and furniture himself. Indeed, the tract of land he purchased included a small piece of ancient woodland, known locally as Grinnton Spinney, which Lurgan reckoned as a fine source of quality timber, and favoured wood gathered there for many of his creations in his new home.

That smudgy drawing I first saw dates from the days of the house's first occupant, drawn by a local socialite who dabbled in the arts. Lewis Staples was a young man about town; the sort who would have been at home in a P.G. Wodehouse novel. However, he was not some brainless drone with money filling in for a lack of aptitude. He had begun decorating his letters and postcards with sketches and watercolours of wherever he was staying. And so, his hosts would be commissioning him to do proper paintings and drawings of their home. By all accounts he was on the verge of becoming a national sensation - judging from the number of invitations and requests he received. He had attended a Halloween ball thrown by Lurgan in October 1910, and produced the charcoal portrait of Malvern House in the days following. Lurgan received the sketch by first post on November 11th. The coroner ruled that Staples died by his own hand by means of drinking a large quantity of lye on November 13th.

What connection this tragic turn of events has to do with Malvern House, indeed if anything at all, is but the first of many unanswered questions.

While the house was a labour of love for Lurgan, his family seems to have had no real affection for the place; for immediately after his death in 1915, his son, Peter, put the house and grounds on the market and made a quick sale. All there is to add is that shortly after his father's passing, the young Lurgan sold off his stake in the family business and enlisted in the army. He was killed in the Battle of the Somme the following year.

Perhaps young Peter saw which way the wind was blowing. The days of the wealthy living on faux country estates at the edge of town were drawing to a close. Times were changing and Wynward was growing rapidly, as twin industries of timber and coal continued to bring prosperity to the county of Redvale. And there was no shortage of wealthy folk who could afford to run a large house.

Hence in 1916, Malvern House passed into the hands of the Campbells; an already affluent young couple, and clearly possessing some shrewd financial acumen.

For they would vastly increase their fortune when they chose to sell off much of the lands attached to the house a few years later. By the 1920s, Wynward was growing and land was in high demand. The couple got an extremely handsome price, and soon new homes would be built on the former Malvern estate. Even Grinnton Spinney was almost completely cut down, save for a small copse that survived as part of the much diminished grounds of Malvern House.

The Campbells lived in the house until 1931, when Edmund Campbell's business collapsed. His wife Susan was forced to sell after her husband was hospitalised. At first he was diagnosed with nervous exhaustion, no doubt a result of the stress of seeing his business empire fall down around his ears. But clearly his troubles ran deeper, for he was later admitted to the Ranson Asylum in Elwin suffering from severe delusions. He would die there in 1935. Local historians are unsure what became of Susan Campbell. For my own part, I can only add that recovering the Visitors' books from the period revealed that Mrs Campbell apparently never visited her husband.

Malvern House's next resident was a retired music hall performer. Peter Cheape had performed as a celebrated ventriloquist act with his dummy Caspian for over thirty years on the northern theatre circuit, but had bid the limelight a fond farewell in 1929 at a sell-out show at the Sunderland Empire. But after settling down in the rural retreat of Wynward, he would still occasionally perform for local events, charity fetes and the like, and would make regular visits with Caspian to the children's ward at the small local hospital.

However, as Mr Cheape's health declined these public appearances gradually petered out. Reportedly, he spent his last years tending the garden, and restoring and restocking with fish an ornamental pond built by Terence Lurgan. In 1939 he was discovered dead in his home. The Coroner's report lists the cause of death as suicide. He had hung himself from an old ash tree in the copse at the bottom of the gardens he loved. The inquest heard he had become increasingly depressed in the last few years, apparently becoming more troubled as his fitness declined and he became increasingly housebound. Friends speculated the increasing stresses on the Home Front were too much for him, and having lost many friends in the Great War he simply could not face living through another. The inquest concluded that the balance of his mind had become disturbed. However, the reason for this learned assumption were never made public, nor reported by the press. However, the original report contains several macabre details that would lead even a casual reader to the assumption that Cheape had suffered some form of mental collapse. For prior to taking his own life, Cheape had also placed a noose around Caspian's neck and hung the dummy on a tree next to him.

One wonders can a house be unlucky? Certainly I think we have all encountered people who had terrible runs of ill fortune, sometimes so pronounced one half jokingly wonders if they have offended some jealous god or other. But do places have their own fortunes? I appreciate that we as humans tend to find patterns in all things - the faces in the fire, the witch in the shadows of the wardrobe. And historians perhaps doubly so. However, I fear most historical scholars would shy away from some of the theories I have entertained.

However, we shall return to my outline of the house's history and the reader can form their own impressions.

Following this tragic incident the house appears to have remained empty for a time, and while one might be tempted to assume it was because of the latest tragedy, other more sanguine reasons seem to be responsible. Cheape died intestate, that is to say he died without a legally valid will. In such cases, efforts are made to trace a suitable beneficiary. In this case, Cheape had a brother who was serving in the military. Letters from the War Office to the council's lawyers tells us that a Sgt. Cheape was serving in the North African theatre, and that correspondence would be forwarded to him when it was possible. But nothing else was forthcoming.

However, before too long life did return to its halls and rooms, prompted by necessity rather than choice. For after some dialogue between government and council, it was agreed that the empty residence be pressed into useful service as temporary accommodation for children to be evacuated from the cities. But these arrangements did not last long, for reasons that remain somewhat obscure.

While examining assorted police incident books, local historians have discovered that about this time the Warren Road area was the source of several complaints. Seven separate residents alleged to have seen small faces peering in through their windows after dark; four of these added criminal damage to plants, fences and walls. When I looked into this matter, I found a letter in the local newspaper that blamed the evacuated children for the night-time mischief. And so one wonders if the same allegations were made to a higher authority which led to the end of Malvern House being used as a refuge for those escaping the Blitz.

In 1944, it appeared that council letters had finally made it to Cheape's brother. I have not found any reply or correspondence, but the Evening Star lists the property for sale in May of that year. Perhaps, understandably, the house did not sell until after hostilities ceased. And so, in late 1945, the Hamilton family took up residence in the old house, but sold the place within twelve months. Again there is no record or clue as to why they sold so quickly.

The house would stand empty again for another few years, and it is a reasonable assumption that the house's price tag was a little high for the austere post war economy. However, thanks to combing the local archives, I did discover another possible reason. I cannot help but think it probable that Malvern House's prospects of finding a new buyer was understandably soured when a local boy, a seven year old named Eustace Pole, was discovered drowned in the ornamental fishpond in October 1947.

In 1949 the house gained a new owner, another retired gentleman, a former bank clerk named Geoffrey Bliss; and apparently he resided there quite happily for five years. However, he too abruptly left in 1955 for pastures fresh. Quite recently, I discovered purely by chance that Geoffrey Bliss was actually a practising occultist. Starting out as a follower of Aleister Crowley and later developing his own system of modern magic, Bliss wrote a series of self-published books throughout the '50s and '60s using the pen-name Andrew Kirke. Whether this has any bearing on the history of Malvern House, it is impossible to say.

But recently, in a sale of rare books, I managed to acquire a tome written by Andrew Kirke; a.k.a. Geoffrey Bliss. Printed in 1963 by True Light Press (itself an operation ran by another minor figure in the British occult scene, Ronald Franklyn) this slim volume was entitled *Obsession and Astral Parasitism*. In it Kirke referenced experiencing a 'curious instance' in which several objects had become 'enmeshed in the local psychic geography' and acted as 'portals for discarnate influences'. These influences apparently manifested according to Kirke as 'shadowy, but grotesque figures wielding a hideous strength.' From what I can tell Bliss moved around the country a lot, seemingly a man who often lived out of a suitcase, so it is unclear as to where he is referring to. However one cannot help assuming it was Malvern House.

It is hard to say exactly when, but the old house did gain a reputation for being haunted. A tempting theory is that it was simply the accumulation of local paranoia over the peeping tom reports, which incidentally had sporadically recurred over the years, coupled with the unfortunate incidents in the house's history that gave rise to strange tales being told about the place.

Alternatively, folklorists have suggested that stories of Malvern House being haunted were simply a continuation of older tales about the Warren Road; the usual sort of folk yarns one finds linked to roads leading out of a town - meetings with monstrous black hounds, travellers chased by witches, and troublesome faeries dwelling in the local woods. However, what is certain is that in 1960 the first proper recorded claim of something strange in Malvern House surfaced. In a locally produced book entitled *Ghosts of Wynward*, one of the tales therein was entitled 'The Haunted Window'. After luridly summarising Campbell's insanity and Cheape's suicide, the story tells how various folks when passing Malvern House at night, presumably in those times when it had stood empty, claimed to see a ghastly, wizened face peering out of the upper windows.

Sadly the book gives no sources for these reports, and other allegedly true reports contained within it are highly suspect. Quite clearly the authors, a husband and wife team named Diggory and Polly Plummer, borrowed plots from several classic ghost stories (local folklorist Eric Able is of the opinion that these alleged reports of wizened faces and strange shapes in the windows of Malvern House are cribbed from 'The Unnamable', a minor tale by HP Lovecraft) and relocated them to the local area to pad out the volume. Hence, it is entirely possible that these tales of terrible visages spooking passers-by were entirely fabricated.

After Geoffrey Bliss had moved onto pastures fresh, the old house passed through several hands in quick succession. A young couple named Ketterley moved in for a short time, followed by a spinster named Telmar who died suddenly not long after taking up residence. The house was then acquired by a developer, with Kirtle & Underland Construction Ltd. submitting plans to the local council to extensively renovate and extend the house. However, the scheme to convert the old building into several luxury apartments came to nothing; and after standing empty once again for a couple of years, the house was back on the market.

It was during that period that Edward Foreshaw gained access to Malvern House, with the view of photographing the original layout and fittings before the developers got to work. Until his death in 1964, Foreshaw created an extensive photographic archive of Wynward, capturing many historic sites and buildings, and methodically documenting the changing times of his home town. After his death, the collection was very kindly donated to the Wynward Library archives; where it forms an important part of the local history records.

He carefully catalogued the entire house, and to my knowledge, these are the only pictures we have of the original interiors of the house. Needless to say it was terribly exciting to see them. Of course, there were many signs of '40s and '50s fashions present, but one could still get a strong impression of how the place would have looked in its Victorian heyday; with many integral features, such as the extensive wood panelling, carved fireplaces and elaborate staircases, untouched by the vagaries of household trends.

However, when examining the individual serial numbers, I noticed that one of the photographs was missing. According to the library archive, the missing print had not been included in the collection when it was donated to them. Seemingly, Mr. Foreshaw had decided not to make this particular picture public.

Fortunately, the chap who originally took charge of the collection was still around - a Mr. Brayburn. He was only too pleased to speak with a fellow local historian, and recalled in detail what he referred to as the palaver over that photograph. Apparently, the picture had caught a ghost. Or at least that is what some claimed. While Foreshaw himself was of the opinion that it was merely a fault in the film, when he held an exhibition of the Malvern pictures, enough folk claimed to see something unearthly that he withdrew it from public display.

According to various recollections of those I could find who had seen the print in question, there was little agreement on what it showed. While all the descriptions tallied well enough in the general details - it showed a gloomy room, sparsely furnished with an occasional table and a large wardrobe; where opinions diverged was regarding the supposed spectral figure. Some remarked on a small figure slumped on a chair, but others complained of a menacing shadow. Some swore there was a troubling figure lurking by the wardrobe. However, whatever the picture showed, people who had seen the photograph were united on one front - nobody liked it. Apparently, Foreshaw destroyed both the print and the negative in early 1964; not long before his death later that year.

In late 1963, the Hardie family moved into Malvern House; a well-to-do couple with a young son. Having relocated from Leeds, the Hardies did not know the house's history and were unconcerned about the tales of haunted windows and the like. Indeed, for the next couple of years all seemed well. However, in 1965, the house hit the headlines again - the Hardies' son, Douglas, had disappeared. A lengthy search for the missing ten year old was mounted, but turned up nothing. Events would take a darker turn when the police took his father in for questioning. Clive Hardie protested his innocence, but several witnesses had come forward testifying that they had observed him having heated arguments with his son. Furthermore, there were reports of bangs and screams in the house in the weeks preceding the lad's disappearance. He was released without charge, but the notion that he had killed his boy was further cemented in the public's mind when it was revealed that his wife, Joy, had left him shortly after Douglas's disappearance.

Ultimately, the police would concur with popular opinion, but when arriving to arrest Mr. Hardie they received no answer at the front door - despite signs of residence such as lighted lamps and officers reporting seeing movements within the house - and were forced to break into the premises, only to discover Hardie hanged inside a large wardrobe. A piece of paper found at the scene, taken as a suicide note by the authorities, simply read: 'Torment no longer.' With no body ever found, whether the boy had been murdered or simply ran away from an unhappy home, we will never know. Incidentally, the police found no sign of any other persons in the house.

Unsurprisingly, after these troubling events, Malvern House remained empty. Several times the police were called after lights and figures were seen inside. No arrests were ever made. Thanks to some campaigning by local residents, the council eventually acquired the property with a mooted scheme to resurrect the former development plans. Funding for the project proved to be somewhat elusive, but at least the building was maintained from falling into complete disrepair. A certain proportion of these costs were met by the council auctioning off the sundry furnishings of the house. Furniture, carpets, and several objet d'art which had been resident in the house since its earliest days went under the hammer. Local historians protested, but there was no arguing with the accountants. It is still a source of consternation among local historical groups that the auction was conducted in such a makeshift fashion that no detailed catalog was produced and no proper records of the sales kept. It is alleged by those who know about these kind of things that the Foreshaw sequence of photographs show the house possessed several valuable antiques, and there is considerable speculation on the prints and artwork one can dimly see adorning the walls.

I often wonder about where the house's holdings ended up. Do any survive still, and what stories could they tell?

For a brief time, Wynward Council attempted to use Malvern House as out-of-town office space. However, according to the council minutes, after a trial period it was felt the premises were 'unsuitable.' Curiously the written report appears to have been lost or misplaced, so no further details are available.

In 1971, a fire broke out. Fortunately, the blaze was brought under control before it could consume any neighbouring properties, but the damage to Malvern House was extensive. Little remained after the council cleared away the rubble and charred timbers. Just the low remains of collapsed walls jutting from the overgrown ground like the remnants of decayed teeth. Investigators initially considered arson as a cause, for several witnesses reported seeing a short figure in the grounds just before the blaze began. However, no trace of an artificial accelerant was discovered; leading the official report to conclude that in all likelihood the fire began as a result of an electrical fault. Of course, that did not stop a dubious rumour beginning that claimed Douglas Hardie had returned to take revenge.

The site was declared a hazard to the public and secured by the council. The land was later sold off and has passed through the hands of several developers. Numerous building projects have been announced over the years, but nothing has ever come of them. No one seemed to have any luck with the place, and some older residents joke that Malvern House had been built on the site of an ancient Indian burial ground.

So, to this day, the site stands empty, still enclosed behind the old stone wall and rusted iron gates. But stories still surface now and again of lights appearing and odd figures seen walking through the overgrown grounds. It is completely out of bounds to the public, and requests by local ghost hunting groups to hold vigils there have been refused. Officially, the site is deemed 'hazardous,' an opinion with which I concur, although not for the same reasons as the local Health & Safety department.

But the house still haunts me. I suspect it always will. I often dream I'm back in the long winter of 1974. Travelling through the dark, approaching those wrought iron gates that loom so ominously in my childhood memories, and glimpsing Malvern House; alone and silent, waiting behind its veil of gloomy trees. Sometimes, I am not in Dad's old Cortina, but alone on the street, approaching the gates with slow inevitable steps that crunch on the frosted leaves.

I have considered taking all my files and photos, the cuttings and letters, this whole patchworks of documents concerning Malvern House, and weaving them into a book. If I had a little less integrity, I feel sure that its history could be spun into a bestseller; like they did with that house in Amityville. It could certainly put the town on the map again; although I am not sure it would be wise to invite a stream of pilgrims to the site of Malvern House's grave.

I have considered just burning the lot; particularly since the dreams have become more frequent.

I feel like I am done with Malvern House, indeed with this town. I should pack up and move, move far away. Leave the unanswered questions for other hands to solve. And there will be others, of that I am sure. The house sings a song of its own, calling you home.

But there is one question I cannot let go - one that pins me on its hook. When we were trundling passed in dad's old Cortina, Malvern House was burnt to the ground and the ruins choked in ivy. So, if I had just imagined a house beyond the ancient gates - as children are supposedly wont to do, how did I recognise it so clearly in Staples' charcoal sketch?

If I can find the answer, will the dreams stop? If I cannot, will it not matter how much distance I place between myself and this town? Even if I am on the other side of the world, will I still be walking along that freezing street, the leaves crunching, the frost glistening, a squat figure in a lighted window, the gates slowly opening...

On my desk in a large manilla envelope is a parish magazine printed in Elwin in 1959. I looked long and hard for this particular edition, for it contains the long reproduction of the missing Foreshaw picture. I am afraid to look. Maybe the photo will be too blurry to see anything at all.

Perhaps when I turn the page and see for myself, a spell will be broken; and I'll be free to move on - maybe even move away. However, what I fear is seeing the same figure who now nightly stands at the end of my bed...

Interlude

Mr. Moon's investigation into the troublesome history of Malvern House has inspired me to share with you a little of the haunting history of my old comprehensive school, Easthampstead Park, in Bracknell, Berkshire.

Long before the building I knew was completed, there was a royal hunting lodge on the grounds, where Edward III and his blue-blooded cronies rode out from to kill deer for sport. If a long line of game-keepers are to be believed, the boot - or should that be hoof? - has been on the other foot for seven centuries; for all of them swore on the Bible that they saw Eddie the 3rd running for his life - fool doesn't even know he's dead - chased by a peryton (the head, neck, forelegs and antlers of a stag, and the plumage, wings and hindquarters of a

large bird).

One hundred and fifty nine years later, he was joined by a second Royal: Catherine of Aragon. She spent a miserable few years at Easthampstead Park, waiting for news of her husband's attempt to divorce her when his randy eye turned to Anne Boleyn. Her spirit has been seen devouring a life-size sculpture of Henry VIII made out of marzipan in the bushes close to where the school's tennis courts were built in 1972.

Every 30th of May that falls on a Saturday - the day and date of his death, Alexander Pope is seen on stilts washing the first floor windows. He's due again in 2020.

In the late 19th century, Arthur Hill, 6th Marquess of Downshire, paid for a miniature railway to be built so he could ride a choo-choo train around the estate dishing out wine gums to the needy. He died in 1918, after his shoe laces were tied together by his secret Socialist manservant and he tripped head over heels out of the First Class Carriage and into the beyond. Since 1955, his ghost has been seen hovering in a sitting position - no ghost train around him - as he travels at 40 MPH along the route the railway ran before the track was pulled up, melted down, and recycled as coffin nails.

During World War II, part of the mansion was allocated to pupils from St. Paul's School. They were sent there to escape the London Blitz, but found themselves in the thick of it when a Heinkel He 177 was forced to make an emergency landing on the mile long driveway. They launched a conker attack at the cockpit window; which, thankfully, impressed the Luftwaffe bomber crew sufficiently for the Kapitän not to give the order to turn the MG 81 on them. Nevertheless, their bombardment backfired - literally - when one of the conkers bounced off the fuselage and toe-tagged its thrower. If it had been an ordinary conker, Spotty Herbert would've probably pulled through. But it was as hard as a bullet - having received a double coating of McCormick's Iron Glue. Spotty shows up every October 1st to play the conker game with anyone who can stomach the sight of the hole in his head. However, as I found out for myself in '88, it always ends in stalemate; as, like him, his conker is an apparition - so his opponent's conker passes straight through it (and visa-versa). But, on the bright side, his skin is spotless because acne does not exist in the afterlife.

8

Reading Vince Stadon's story has caused my fear of small islands - which I thought I'd well and truly sunk to the bottom of my memory pool - to bubble back up to the surface...

When I was six, my mother and I were in a dinghy that was drifting out to sea, due to a crab's entanglement in the outboard motor. We transferred onto the craggy surface of a skerry (small rocky island) and waved frantically for help to passers by on the shore.

Luckily, it worked. But while we waited to be rescued, I heard an irate male voice say: "Get off my island."

I know my mother heard it too because she squeezed my hand tightly and moved us over to the other side of the outcrop.

When the coastguard arrived, the one who helped us into the lifeboat said: "That's odd. The person who rang us said there were three people stranded out here. And I could have sworn I saw three myself when I spotted you from the harbour."

STEEPE HOLM

by Vince Stadon

There was a ghost at the wake.

Well, there's a ghost at every wake. The lingering presence of the dearly departed, celebrated in tears and song and drink; treasured memories shared like gifts.

But at this wake, there really was a ghost - of sorts. Tom Matthews felt it as it drifted round the room, from person to person. The ghost was in their eyes when they looked at him, on their lips as they whispered about him. Because where Matthews went, so did the ghost. Julius Ondon. Matthews could never escape from him. Especially here, in sight of Steepe Holm.

There was an open coffin, which took him by surprise because he had not expected, nor been prepared, to see her. Jenny. The first woman he ever loved. The woman he had married, all those decades ago. She looked old: another surprise. But then, he had only ever seen her as a young woman. They were divorced at thirty-five. Seeing her with white hair was a jolt. She'd had such vibrant red hair when he knew her. Red Jenny, they called her. Wild and beautiful Red Jenny. She had been a catch. He had been very lucky to have her; and very stupid to lose her.

Matthews realised he was crying, and he was embarrassed. He wiped away the tears and moved to a corner of the room to be by himself. He sat in a creaky old chair and got himself together. A nip from his hip flask helped. He could have helped himself to the free wine and sherry, but he preferred the hard stuff. Wine and sherry had been more Jenny's taste.

"Tom?"

He looked up. An attractive young woman stood before him. A hint of red in her hair. He tried to place her.

"Mel," she said, introducing herself. "Jenny and Brian's daughter."

"Of course," he said, and smiled. Jenny had remarried and she and her second husband Brian had had kids. Two, if he remembered right.

"Thank you for coming," said Mel. "I know how difficult it can be, for exes. Most wouldn't have bothered."

"I felt I had to see her, to say goodbye." Matthews hoped she couldn't smell the alcohol on his breath, and wished he'd grabbed a glass of wine to use as a prop. "I'm sorry she's gone."

"Thank you, she's at peace. We appreciate you coming."

"We couldn't have stopped you," said a man moving closer to stand by Mel. He put his arm around her shoulder.

"My brother, Mark," she said, introducing him to Matthews.

"Off back after this are you?" Mark was the opposite of his sister. Where Mel was slim, attractive and pleasant, Mark was stocky, gruff and accusatory. He had a rugby player's build.

"No, actually I thought I'd stay a few days," said Matthews, enjoying the scowl that bruised Mark's face.

"We don't want any of your nonsense. You won't be upsetting people, like before."

"What?" Matthews was already tired of this moron. He'd dealt with many of his type over the years, men too quick with their fists and too slow with their brains. "Now look, I'm just here to pay my respects and spend a few days sightseeing, not that it's any bloody business of yours."

"In this weather?"

Matthews shrugged. "I brought an umbrella."

"Well, I don't want you dredging up the past, upsetting Mel. All that mumbo jumbo ghost stuff. Julius Ondon, the madman of Steepe Holm. Utter rubbish."

"Mark, stop being rude to Tom."

"It's alright," said Matthews.

"Gave mum nightmares you did," said Mark, raising his voice. He was upset, and was escalating the situation. Matthews sighed. Moron. "She still talked about it, she was still scared. Crying in the night, afraid to look out to sea. That was all 'cause of you!"

"Mark!" Mel snapped at him, pulled him sharply by the arm. "I'm sorry, Tom. Mark's a bit upset."

"It's okay," said Matthews. "It's perfectly okay."

Matthews left shortly after, hurrying away from the community centre, aware that everybody was watching him. He had lied about having an umbrella, so he pulled his collar up, and sank his hands deep into his pockets, as he walked along the lonely promenade. The rain was almost horizontal in the sea wind. He remembered the first winter he had experienced here in Washbourne, and how Jenny, local born and bred, had teased him he was soft for complaining about the cold and the rain. She had loved all the seasons, all types of weather. She had looked good in any type of clothing, but he remembered how especially lovely she looked in winter wear, red cheeks and long scarf, and knitted bobble hat. He felt an ache for her.

Matthews realised he had stopped walking, and that he was staring out to sea. His clothes were soaked through. The grey sea was veiled in a wash of mist, but Matthews could just about make it out - the hump of land known as Steepe Holm. He could remember the very first time he had heard of it. He had been standing just about where he was stood now, Jenny at his side, rain lashing down. They had been buying groceries, he recalled.

"What's that?" he had asked her, pointing to the mist-drenched island.

"Oh, that's Steepe Holm. Supposedly haunted," she had said.

"Really? Have you been there?"

"Nope. Nobody goes there."

It didn't look too far out to sea. Matthews was pretty sure he could swim it, on a good day. "What's there?"

"Nothing's there."

"No wildlife? Place like that, out at sea, no rare birds?"

"Nothing. What are you doing?"

Matthews was feeding a two pence coin into the seaside telescope. "Just taking a scoob."

"You won't see anything."

And at first he didn't see anything. Just a barren island. But just as his money was about to run out and his view shut off, he thought he glimpsed movement. Something standing up. A man. Matthews almost jumped back.

"What's the matter?"

"Nothing," he said. "Just thought I saw the ghost." He tried to keep his voice light, make a joke of it. But neither of them had found it funny.

He was staying at the Sea View guesthouse, a drab and unwelcoming B.&B. that looked as if it hadn't been decorated since the 90's, and smelled of damp, particularly along the second floor corridor, where he had been roomed. Time was, he could have booked somewhere considerably better; these days, The Sea View was all he could really afford on his pension, and at least there was the promise of a hot breakfast every morning. His room had an excellent sea view, as the name of the place had promised. The place seemed empty, but there were noises coming from the room next door: creaks and thuds, and sometimes laughter.

Matthews stood at the window as night fell and the moon rose over the sea. Steepe Holm was out there. And he couldn't help but feel that there was a dark shape, a man, looking back at him.

He had been fascinated by Steepe Holm, particularly because there seemed to be so little mention of it. For a seaside resort, you'd think the Washbourne Tourist Board would be promoting it widely as a place of interest, but it was almost as if the island was a dirty secret that they'd rather nobody knew about. The island appeared on no postcards or other merchandising, and it barely registered on local maps. It was haunted, the locals said. Best not go there. Here, have an ice cream, and have you been on the pier? Even Jenny, so usually proud of her hometown, had not had much to say about it.

"There's two other Steepe Holms, apparently," was all she had said. They were painting the nursery together. They still had hope back then. "One of them's down south in the Bristol Channel, I think, though it doesn't have the 'e' on the end. Other one's off the Scottish coast, probably has a 'Mc' in the name." Matthews had wondered why she was being evasive, but he knew he had to shake off such thoughts. He had to trust her, had to learn how to be married. And, he hoped, one day to be a father.

The call had come a few nights later. Matthews remembered the exact date - October 12th 1985. They were painting the woodwork, listening to the radio, having a giggle. He'd sighed when the telephone rang, put down his paintbrush, wiped his hands, and picked up the receiver.

"D.I. Matthews."

"Sir, it's D.S. Eddings."

"What is it, Eddings?"

"Missing girl, sir. Possible kidnapping."

"How old?"

"Twenty, sir." There was a pause.

"What aren't you saying, Sergeant?"

"Sir, it's Johnny Cook's wife."

"Christ. I'll be right there."

Johnny Cook was a rising star in the light entertainment world, had toured with famous names, was being touted as the next big thing. He was headlining a variety show on the pier, winter season, honing his act for television. Matthews sat next to him as the spiky-haired man chain-smoked in his hotel room - the best suite in the Grand Hotel. No expense spared for Johnny.

"Tell me what's happened," said Matthews. "I know you've told the other detectives, but I want you to tell me."

"She's gone! My Betsy. Gone - he took her!" Johnny Cook was wearing too much aftershave and fake tan.

"Who took her, Mr. Cook?"

"The fisherman. You gotta go after him!"

"What fisherman?"

"I dunno - he pulled up to the beach in his rowboat. I didn't see much of him - his back was to me, and Betsy was crying."

"Why was Betsy crying?"

Johnny Cook tried a cheeky smile, but it came out as a leer. "We'd had a row, stupid cow thought I was knocking around with one of the girls from the show."

"You were arguing here, in your hotel suite?"

"No, in a pub down by the beach - The Seahorse."

Matthews looked at D.S. Eddings. "Rough pub, sir," said the Detective Sergeant, "mainly frequented by boat crew."

Matthews nodded. "Go on, Mr. Cook," he said.

"Lost me temper, didn't I? One too many and I see red sometimes. And she was just going on and on..."

"You hit her?" Matthews kept the revulsion from his voice.

"Just a slap or two. She runs off! And it's howling out there, rain and sleet."

"You went after her?"

"Yeah, after a few minutes - I was having a laugh with some of the lads. When I did, I see her walking along the beach, and I call after her. That's when I heard the rowing."

"Rowing?" Matthews couldn't believe a rowing boat would be put to use on a night like this.

"I see this boat coming in to the beach, and Betsy's stood there, looking at it. I start to run, but trip over, flat on my face. I hear Betsy screaming and shouting, and I get up and look and she's gone, and the boat's out to sea again, fisherman is rowing away like the devil."

"You saw your wife on the boat?"

"No, but it was bleedin' obvious she was on it - where else could she be? One minute she's stood there, next minute she's screaming her head off and then she's gone!"

"You heard her screaming and shouting. Could you make out any words?"

Johnny Cook looked surprised by the question. He took a long drag of the cigarette as he thought about it. "Yeah. Yeah, now you comes to mention it. I thought I heard her shout a name."

"What name?"

"Something like, 'Julius Ondon'."

"Christ," said D.S. Eddings.

Remarkably, Johnny Cook's story seemed to check out. The Coast Guard searched for three days, while Matthews led a house-to-house, and personally walked every inch of Steepe Holm. Witnesses at The Seahorse confirmed Cook's account. A search of the beach turned up Betsy's bracelet, which could have been pulled off her wrist in a struggle. Cook was detained and questioned, blood and D.N.A. samples taken, lawyers called in. The London papers started sniffing around, meaning the story briefly made national news. Betsy Cook was never found, and Johnny Cook never made the big time. Matthews read of his suicide a decade or so later. Case unsolved. His first big case as Detective Inspector at his new posting. His first failure. Because Matthews had too many questions, and he wouldn't stop asking them. He couldn't let it go. At night, next to Jenny, he dreamed often of a rowboat on a choppy sea. It was coming in fast as the rain lashed down, the man in the boat powering his oars into the water, and up out, and down again and up, a relentless rhythm. He had his back to Matthews, watching helplessly from the shore, but Matthews knew the man was coming for his wife. Julius Ondon was coming to take Jenny away to Steepe Holm. Matthews would wake up screaming.

The stink of damp was getting worse, and Matthews couldn't bear to spend much time in the guest house. He asked if he could have a different room, on the ground floor, but the proprietor, Mrs. Black, told him all the rooms were occupied. Matthews hadn't seen a single soul, not even a maid, and treated this information with suspicion. The only sign of life he had detected in the building came from the noises made by the man in the room next door.

"Who is in Room 7? Next to mine?"

"One of me regulars, comes here every year." Mrs. Black looked to be in her fifties, overweight and grey-faced, with horn-rimmed glasses and a permanent scowl.

"Haven't seen him at breakfast?" Matthews was trying to be polite.

"Keeps to himself. Unlike some."

Matthews took the hint, and went for a walk.

In winter, the tourist shops were boarded up, and Washbourne looked like a ghost town. Matthews recognised few of the new shops and pubs. The Seahorse was now a Wetherspoons, and most other properties were either pawn shops, bookies, or arcades filled with school kids. He was glad to see the church on the hill where Jenny and he had been wed. He went inside and lit a candle for her, and sat for a while, sipping from his flask and thinking.

"That name. Julius Ondon."

"Yeah." D.S. Eddings said, loosening his tie. Matthews had noticed he only did that when he was uncomfortable.

"You recognised it."

"Old legend. Local. Hold up..." D.S. Eddings rummaged through his desk drawer, and produced a small dog-eared paperback book. He handed it to Matthews.

Matthews read the title. *This Spectral Isle: Hauntings of Britain.* There was a bookmark marking a page of interest. Matthews flicked to it, found a passage highlighted in pencil: 'Steepe Holm, off the Norfolk Coast, is a Carboniferous Limestone island, uninhabited since the Middle Ages except for briefly during World War Two, when the island was used by the British Navy as a radar station. The station was in usage for only a few months before it was decommissioned because of persistent unexplained technical failures, and reports of an Anglo-Saxon ghost, believed to be Julius Ondon, a fisherman from the nearby coastal resort town of Washbourne. Ondon was suspected of murdering his wife and was imprisoned on Steepe Holm, where he starved to death. He is supposed to have sworn vengeance on the people of Washbourne.'

"That's it?"

D.S. Eddings shrugged. "That's all I've ever known."

Matthews checked the publication date. "This came out in 1950. Any mention of this Julius Ondon before that?"

"No, not that I've ever seen. But my mother talked about

him. She and other women she knew had heard the story. But that was a long, long time ago; I aint heard the name since."

"Then how did Mrs. Betsy Cook know the name? And if Johnny Cook is making it all up, how did he know the name?"

D.S. Eddings shrugged again. This was way outside his usual duties as a detective. In Washbourne, the most common crimes were shoplifting and public affray due to being drunk and disorderly. "Do you believe him, sir? Johnny Cook?"

"I believe he's telling the truth as he knows it to be, which is not the same as believing his story. I keep coming back to the question of the boat - if there was one - being rowed ashore exactly as Betsy Cook got to that precise spot on the beach. What are the odds of that?"

"Yeah. It's just like the other times."

Matthews felt his blood go cold. "What other times?"

Seventeen women. All supposedly kidnapped, at night, from Washbourne beach, and never seen again. Matthews couldn't believe what he was reading - a ragbag collection of newspaper clippings and garbled incident reports, collected in a dusty folder. The most recent was a Missing Persons report filed on December 19th, 1956. Mrs. Cynthia Paxton was last seen by her husband, Frederick Paxton, and her younger sister, Glenys Reed, running along the beach at around 10 PM, before she disappeared. Witnesses say they thought they heard the sounds of a boat rowing ashore. That was it. No follow-up. Underneath the report was a photo. of a young woman in a naval uniform, stood proudly on the deck of a ship. On the reverse was written: *Second Officer Daphne Seldon, HMS Valiant, 1941. Missing from Washbourne/Steepe Holm, December, 1943.*' In all, there were seventeen recorded instances of women vanishing from the beach. Plus a strange account of a sermon delivered by the Reverend Arbunter, one winter Sunday in 1766, in which he claimed Washbourne was under the grip of an evil spirit named Julius Ondon. Matthews was angry. Why hadn't he been shown this file straight away? D.S. Eddings could offer only a shrug, saying it was just local mumbo jumbo, like his mother said. Nobody took it seriously. But Matthews did. Matthews took it very seriously.

Back at The Sea View, Matthews tried to sleep off the alcohol he had consumed. He'd finished off two bottles whilst in the church, remembering. The warden had to practically throw Matthews out of the church, explaining that it was his duty to shut the doors for the night, and informing Matthews of a nearby doss house that took in the homeless. Matthews laughed, remembering. Stupid idiot had thought he was homeless! A drunk old tramp with nowhere to go. What a come down from the bright and promising young detective inspector he had once been, newly married to the prettiest girl in town. He laughed again, but soon stopped when he realised he wasn't laughing alone.

Matthews sat upright, which he immediately regretted. Head-spinning, he tried to get off the bed, but he collapsed and the last thing he heard before he lost consciousness was the man next door laughing at him.

The next afternoon, Matthews walked along the seafront, glad of the rain. He should have showered, he knew; or at least changed his clothes. But he had to get out of that room. The damp was getting so bad that water was pooling outside Room 7.

Matthews stood for a long while, looking out to sea and to Steepe Holm. He remembered the first time he had been on the island, searching every stone for signs of Betsy Cook. The island was nothing more than rock and mud. There was nothing on it, no buildings of any sort, no features of interest, nothing. Nothing grew there apart from weeds. No birds settled there. The place was a desolate hellhole, lashed by the sea and the rain. But Matthews was convinced there was something there, some clue he was missing.

"Where are you going?" Jenny had asked him one night.

"Work," he had said. "Go back to sleep." There was a distance between them now. She wasn't happy, and he felt bad. Once he solved the case, he would make her happy again. They would have a baby. Go on holiday. He would cut down on his drinking.

He had bought a boat. Second hand, in need of repair and a lick of paint, but Matthews hadn't cared; the boat was seaworthy, that was all that mattered. Jenny need never know. He'd make up the money somehow. Overtime, or a second job. He rowed to Steepe Holm. At first it was every now and again, when he had an idea of what to look for - he took a metal detector once, hoping to unearth Second Officer Daphne Seldon's long buried W.R.E.N. badge. But soon he was going there most nights, pretending a call had come in from work. He felt a desperate need to be there, on Steepe Holm, even though it was exhausting him. The rowing, the lack of sleep, the drinking - it was taking it out of him. One night, his boat capsized and he nearly drowned. He managed to right the boat and climb aboard, scared and tired, and let the boat get carried to Steepe Holm, where he slept. He was off sick with hypothermia for a week. Jenny was desperately worried for him, but he assured her all would be alright. He just had to solve the case.

Feeling weak, Matthews found a cafe and slumped into a seat at a window table. The heating was on full blast, and the radio was playing chart music.

"Are you alright, Tom? You look dreadful."

He looked up. Mel was stood before him, wearing a pinny.

"Hello, Mel. Yes, I'm fine. Could I have some tea, please?"

"Yes, of course. I must say I'm really surprised to see you here."

"Why?"

"I thought you said you'd only be staying for a few days."

"Yes...?" He was confused.

"Have you come back again? Did you go home a week ago?"

"A week ago?"

"Mum's funeral."

He felt a lurch in his stomach. He'd been here a week? Where had the time gone? Why couldn't he remember? Mel was looking very worried. He had to reassure her all was okay. "Sorry. Mind like a sieve these days. Yes, I just popped back to take some photos for the book."

"The book?"

"I'm writing about the case. Julius Ondon."

"Oh. I'll get your tea."

She surprised him by bringing him cake, and sitting with him. He fished in his pockets, produced a handful of change, but she said she wouldn't hear of it - you don't charge family.

"I meant to say sorry about Mark. At the funeral. He was rude to you, and that wasn't nice."

"That's okay."

"She talked about you, you know, mum. She said how happy she was in the beginning; the two of you getting married, buying a house together. How proud she was to have got you here from London."

Matthews smiled. "She was very beautiful. We were happy until he came along."

"Who?"

"I sometimes think he took her from me, you know. And maybe I'd find her again, if I solved the case."

"Tom?"

"See, I'm convinced he took her there."

"Tom, please stop crying…"

"To Steepe Holm."

"Tom, please sit down, I think you need help. Let me fetch somebody…"

Matthews smiled. It was okay. Everything would be okay. He left the cafe and walked away, wondering what he had missed. He wished he still had his case notes. He'd turned the nursery into a makeshift office, had drawings of Julius Ondon pinned to the wall - made by a police sketch artist talking on the phone to Johnny Cook in London. Jenny had been upset, but he promised her that there would be a baby one day. He was just using the room for now, so that it wouldn't go to waste.

The boss had called him into his office.

"What the hell is this?" He shoved a piece of paper at Matthews. It was one of the WANTED posters of Julius Ondon.

"It's the best description we have, sir. Just the back of his head, but that cloak and hood is distinctive, somebody might recogn--"

"For Christ's sake, have you gone mad? You've put these things up everywhere!"

"Sir, I think--"

"Shut up, Matthews, I don't care what you think. You're scaring people, causing a panic. You're not even on the case any more, so what the hell are you doing with this nonsense?"

"I'm sure I can solve it, sir. If we can find Julius Ondon…"

"The Anglo-Saxon ghost? Listen to yourself! And take a look in the mirror sometime, you're a disgrace. You're suspended from duty, Matthews. I've had enough of you. We've all had enough of you."

"Sir, I..."

"Get out!"

"Get out!"

Matthews stopped in his tracks. Mrs. Black was shouting at him. Old hag. What did she want? He just needed to go to his room, get some sleep.

"I told you, get out!"

"I'm going to my room. Leave me alone."

"You don't have a room here!"

"What?" Stupid old woman. Of course he had a room. He'd only checked in yesterday.

"You ain't welcome here. Get out, I tell you!"

He ignored her and made his way upstairs, searching his pockets for his key. He couldn't find it, assumed he'd left it in his room. Mind like a sieve these days. He heard the man laughing in Room 7 and it angered him. Everybody was laughing at him these days, telling him to get out, or drop the case, or that they wanted a divorce. Everybody was trying to stop him from doing his job. He'd had enough. He hammered on the door.

"You won't stop me! You'll never stop me!"

The man inside was laughing. It had to be Julius Ondon.

Matthews shoulder-barged the door. It hurt like hell, and the door didn't budge. The man laughed at him.

"Stop it, you idiot!" A man grabbed him, pulled him away from the door. Matthews was surprised to see it was a police constable. A big chap, built for rugby. The face was familiar. Mrs. Black was at the top of the stairs, looking ashen.

"Help me get in this room, Constable," he said. "There's a man in there - he's kidnapped a woman."

"What are you on about? Get away, Matthews!"

"Do as I say, Constable. That's an order!"

"Right, you leave me no choice. I'm arresting you on the charge of public affray. You do not have to say anything, but anything you do say may be used against you."

"I know you, don't I? You're Mark. Jenny's son."

"Yes, and I warned you, you stupid sod. You're coming with me."

The door to Room 7 opened as the policeman led Matthews away, and a scared old woman peered out.

Matthews understood now. "Of course," he muttered. "Of course he wouldn't be in there - he was just playing with my mind. He's where he always is - he's on Steepe Holm."

Matthews was released the next morning. He felt better for a good night's sleep, and he felt full of purpose. The sea air was invigorating. He felt young again, sharp, glad to be back on the case. He sat on the seafront all day, waiting for dark. Then when it was time he made his way down to the beach and he stood in the spot where Betsy Cook had stood, and the boat was waiting for him; as he knew it would be. He rowed out to sea - to Steepe Holm.

Witnesses could not identify the man in the boat with him.

9.

I love the word CREEPY... Don't you?

'Creep' first appears in Old English as the verb crēopan - to move the body near or along the ground as a reptile or insect does. It was first used to describe a feeling of dread or revulsion in 1831; and, eighteen years later, as causing a creeping sensation of the skin:

"She was constantly complaining of the cold, and of its occasioning a visitation in her back which she called the creeps." --- Charles Dickens, DAVID COPPERFIELD

So collections of CREEPY stories released close to Christmas have their roots (or should that be tentacles?) in esteemed company indeed - the author who started the tradition of telling ghost stories at Christmas, no less! Therefore, it's only fitting that one of his CREEPY stories is included in the collection.

THE TRIAL FOR MURDER

by Charles Dickens

When the murder was first discovered, no suspicion fell - or I ought rather to say, for I cannot be too precise in my facts, it was nowhere publicly hinted that any suspicion fell - on the man who was afterwards brought to trial. As no reference was at that time made to him in the newspapers, it is obviously impossible that any description of him can at that time have been given in the newspapers. It is essential that this fact be remembered.

Unfolding at breakfast my morning paper, containing the account of that first discovery, I found it to be deeply interesting, and I read it with close attention. I read it twice, if not three times. The discovery had been made in a bedroom, and, when I laid down the paper, I was aware of a flash - rush - flow - I do not know what to call it; no word I can find is satisfactorily descriptive, in which I seemed to see that bedroom passing through my room, like a picture impossibly painted on a running river. Though almost instantaneous in its passing, it was perfectly clear; so clear that I distinctly, and with a sense of relief, observed the absence of the dead body from the bed.

It was in no romantic place that I had this curious sensation, but in chambers in Piccadilly, very near to the corner of St. James's Street. It was entirely new to me. I was in my easy-chair at the moment, and the sensation was accompanied with a peculiar shiver which started the chair from its position. I went to one of the windows (the room is on the second floor) to refresh my eyes with the moving objects down in Piccadilly. It was a bright autumn morning, and the street was sparkling and cheerful. The wind was high. As I looked out, it brought down from the Park a quantity of fallen leaves, which a gust took, and whirled into a spiral pillar. As the pillar fell and the leaves dispersed, I saw two men on the opposite side of the way, going from West to East. They were one behind the other. The foremost man often looked back over his shoulder. The second man followed him, at a distance of some thirty paces, with his right hand menacingly raised. First, the singularity and steadiness of this threatening gesture in so public a thoroughfare attracted my attention; and next, the more remarkable circumstance that nobody heeded it. Both men threaded their way among the other passengers with a smoothness hardly consistent even with the action of walking on a pavement; and no single creature, that I could see, gave them place, touched them, or looked after them. In passing before my windows, they both stared up at me. I saw their two faces very distinctly, and I knew that I could recognise them anywhere. Not that I had consciously noticed anything very remarkable in either face, except that the man who went first had an unusually lowering appearance, and that the face of the man who followed him was of the colour of impure wax.

I am a bachelor, and my valet and his wife constitute my whole establishment. My occupation is in a certain Branch Bank, and I wish that my duties as head of a Department were as light as they are popularly supposed to be. They kept me in town that autumn, when I stood in need of change. I was not ill, but I was not well. My reader is to make the most that can be reasonably made of my feeling jaded, having a depressing sense upon me of a monotonous life, and being 'slightly dyspeptic'. I am assured by my renowned doctor that my real state of health at that time justifies no stronger description, and I quote his own from his written answer to my request for it.

As the circumstances of the murder, gradually unravelling, took stronger and stronger possession of the public mind, I kept them away from mine by knowing as little about them as was possible in the midst of the universal excitement. But I knew that a verdict of Wilful Murder had been found against the suspected murderer, and that he had been committed to Newgate for trial. I also knew that his trial had been postponed over one Sessions of the Central Criminal Court, on the ground of general prejudice and want of time for the preparation of the defence. I may further have known, but I believe I did not, when, or about when, the Sessions to which his trial stood postponed would come on.

My sitting-room, bedroom, and dressing-room, are all on one floor. With the last there is no communication, but through the bedroom. True, there is a door in it, once communicating with the staircase, but a part of the fitting of my bath has been - and had then been for some years - fixed across it. At the same period, and as a part of the same arrangement, - the door had been nailed up and canvased over.

I was standing in my bedroom late one night, giving some directions to my servant before he went to bed. My face was towards the only available door of communication with the dressing-room, and it was closed. My servant's back was towards that door. While I was speaking to him, I saw it open, and a man look in, who very earnestly and mysteriously beckoned to me. That man was the man who had gone second of the two along Piccadilly, and whose face was of the colour of impure wax.

The figure, having beckoned, drew back, and closed the door. With no longer pause than was made by my crossing the bed-room, I opened the dressing-room door, and looked in. I had a lighted candle already in my hand. I felt no inward expectation of seeing the figure in the dressing-room, and I did not see it there.

Conscious that my servant stood amazed, I turned round to him, and said: "Derrick, could you believe that in my cool senses I fancied I saw a --" As I there laid my hand upon his breast, with a sudden start he trembled violently, and said, "O Lord, yes, sir! A dead man beckoning!"

Now I do not believe that this John Derrick, my trusty and at-tached servant for more than twenty years, had any impression whatever of having seen any such figure, until I touched him. The change in him was so startling, when I touched him, that I fully believe he derived his impression in some occult manner from me at that instant.

I bade John Derrick bring some brandy, and I gave him a dram, and was glad to take one myself. Of what had preceded that night's phenomenon, I told him not a single word. Reflecting on it, I was absolutely certain that I had never seen that face before, except on the one occasion in Piccadilly. Comparing its expres-sion when beckoning at the door with its expression when it had stared up at me as I stood at my window, I came to the con-clusion that on the first occasion it had sought to fasten itself upon my memory, and that on the second occasion it had made sure of being immediately remembered.

I was not very comfortable that night, though I felt a cer-tainty, difficult to explain, that the figure would not return. At daylight I fell into a heavy sleep, from which I was awakened by John Derrick's coming to my bedside with a paper in his hand.

This paper, it appeared, had been the subject of an altercation at the door between its bearer and my servant. It was a summons to me to serve upon a Jury at the forthcoming Sessions of the Central Criminal Court at the Old Bailey. I had never before been summoned on such a Jury, as John Derrick well knew. He believed - I am not certain at this hour whether with reason or otherwise - that that class of Jurors were customarily chosen on a lower qualification than mine, and he had at first refused to accept the summons. The man who served it had taken the matter very coolly. He had said that my attendance or non-attendance was nothing to him; there the summons was; and I should deal with it at my own peril, and not at his.

For a day or two I was undecided whether to respond to this call, or take no notice of it. I was not conscious of the slightest mysterious bias, influence, or attraction, one way or other. Of that I am as strictly sure as of every other statement that I make here. Ultimately I decided, as a break in the monotony of my life, that I would go.

The appointed morning was a raw day in the month of November. There was a dense brown fog in Piccadilly, and it became positively black and in the last degree oppressive east of Temple Bar. I found the passages and staircases of the Court House flaringly lighted with gas, and the Court itself similarly illuminated. I think that, until I was conducted by officers into the Old Court and saw its crowded state, I did not know that the Murderer was to be tried that day. I think that, until I was so helped into the Old Court with considerable difficulty, I did not know into which of the two Courts sitting my summons would take me. But this must not be received as a positive assertion, for I am not completely satisfied in my mind on either point.

I took my seat in the place appropriated to Jurors in waiting, and I looked about the Court as well as I could through the cloud of fog and breath that was heavy in it. I noticed the black vapour hanging like a murky curtain outside the great windows, and I noticed the stifled sound of wheels on the straw or tan that was littered in the street; also, the hum of the people gathered there, which a shrill whistle, or a louder song or hail than the rest, occasionally pierced. Soon afterwards the Judges, two in number, entered, and took their seats. The buzz in the Court was awfully hushed. The direction was given to put the Murderer to the bar. He appeared there; and in that same instant, I recognised in him the first of the two men who had gone down Piccadilly.

If my name had been called then, I doubt if I could have answered to it audibly. But it was called about sixth or eighth in the panel, and I was by that time able to say, "Here!" Now, observe. As I stepped into the box, the prisoner, who had been looking on attentively, but with no sign of concern, became violently agitated, and beckoned to his attorney. The prisoner's wish to challenge me was so manifest, that it occasioned a pause, during which the attorney, with his hand upon the dock, whispered with his client, and shook his head. I afterwards had it from that gentleman, that the prisoner's first affrighted words to him were, "At all hazards, challenge that man!" But that, as he would give no reason for it, and admitted that he had not even known my name until he heard it called and I appeared, was not done.

Both on the ground already explained, that I wish to avoid reviving the unwholesome memory of that Murderer, and also because a detailed account of his long trial is by no means indispensable to my narrative, I shall confine myself closely to such incidents in the ten days and nights during which we, the Jury, were kept together, as directly bear on my own curious personal experience. It is in that, and not in the Murderer, that I seek to interest my reader.

I was chosen Foreman of the Jury. On the second morning of the trial, after evidence had been taken for two hours (I heard the church clocks strike), happening to cast my eyes over my brother jurymen, I found an inexplicable difficulty in counting them. I counted them several times, yet always with the same difficulty. In short, I made them one too many.

I touched the brother jurymen whose place was next me, and I whispered to him, "Oblige me by counting us." He looked surprised by the request, but turned his head and counted. "Why," says he, suddenly, "we are Thirt - ; but no, it's not possible. No. We are twelve."

According to my counting that day, we were always right in detail, but in the gross we were always one too many. There was no appearance - no figure - to account for it; but I had now an inward foreshadowing of the figure that was surely coming.

The Jury were housed at the London Tavern. We all slept in one large room on separate tables, and we were constantly in the charge and under the eye of the officer sworn to hold us in safe-keeping. I see no reason for suppressing the real name of that officer. He was intelligent, highly polite, and obliging, and (I was glad to hear) much respected in the City. He had an agreeable presence, good eyes, enviable black whiskers, and a fine sonorous voice. His name was Mr. Harker.

When we turned into our twelve beds at night, Mr. Harker's bed was drawn across the door. On the night of the second day, not being disposed to lie down, and seeing Mr. Harker sitting on his bed, I went and sat beside him, and offered him a pinch of snuff. As Mr. Harker's hand touched mine in taking it from my box, a peculiar shiver crossed him, and he said, "Who is this?"

Following Mr. Harker's eyes, and looking along the room, I saw again the figure I expected - the second of the two men who had gone down Piccadilly. I rose, and advanced a few steps; then stopped, and looked round at Mr. Harker. He was quite unconcerned, laughed, and said in a pleasant way, "I thought for a moment we had a thirteenth juryman, without a bed. But I see it is the moonlight."

Making no revelation to Mr. Harker, but inviting him to take a walk with me to the end of the room, I watched what the figure did. It stood for a few moments by the bedside of each of my eleven brother jurymen, close to the pillow. It always went to the right-hand side of the bed, and always passed out crossing the foot of the next bed. It seemed, from the action of the head, merely to look down pensively at each recumbent figure. It took no notice of me, or of my bed, which was that nearest to Mr. Harker's. It seemed to go out where the moonlight came in, through a high window, as by an aerial flight of stairs.

Next morning at breakfast, it appeared that everybody present had dreamed of the murdered man last night, except myself and Mr. Harker.

I now felt convinced that the second man who had gone down Piccadilly was the murdered man (so to speak), as if it had been borne into my comprehension by his immediate testimony. But even this took place, and in a manner for which I was not at all prepared.

On the fifth day of the trial, when the case for the prosecution was drawing to a close, a miniature of the murdered man, missing from his bedroom upon the discovery of the deed, and afterwards found in a hiding place where the Murderer had been seen digging, was put in evidence. Having been identified by the witness under examination, it was handed up to the Bench, and thence handed down to be inspected by the Jury. As an officer in a black gown was making his way with it across to me, the figure of the second man who had gone down Piccadilly impetuously started from the crowd, caught the miniature from the officer, and gave it to me with his own hands, at the same time saying, in a low and hollow tone - "I was younger then, and my face was not then drained of blood." It also came between me and the brother juryman to whom I would have given the miniature, and between him and the brother juryman to whom he would have given it, and so passed it on through the whole of our number, and back into my possession. Not one of them, however, detected this.

At table, and generally when we were shut up together in Mr. Harker's custody, we had from the first naturally discussed the day's proceedings a good deal. On that fifth day, the case for the prosecution being closed, and we having that side of the question in a completed shape before us, our discussion was more animated and serious. Among our number was a vestryman - the densest idiot I have ever seen at large - who met the plainest evidence with the most preposterous objections, and who was sided with by two flabby parochial parasites; all three impanelled from a district so delivered over to Fever that they ought to have been upon their own trial for five hundred Murders. When these mischievous blockheads were at their loudest, which was towards midnight, while some of us were already preparing for bed, I again saw the murdered man. He stood grimly behind them, beckoning to me. On my going towards them, and striking into the conversation, he immediately retired. This was the beginning of a separate series of appearances, confined to that long room in which we were confined. Whenever a knot of my brother jurymen laid their heads together, I saw the head of the murdered man among theirs. Whenever their comparison of notes was going against him, he would solemnly and irresistibly beckon to me.

It will be borne in mind that down to the production of the miniature, on the fifth day of the trial, I had never seen the Appearance in Court. Three changes occurred now that we entered on the case for the defence. Two of them I will mention together, first. The figure was now in Court continually, and it never there addressed itself to me, but always to the person who was speaking at the time. For instance: the throat of the murdered man had been cut straight across. In the opening speech for the defence, it was suggested that the deceased might have cut his own throat. At that very moment, the figure, with its throat in that dreadful condition (this it had concealed before), stood at the speaker's elbow, motioning across and across its windpipe, now with the right hand, now with the left, vigorously suggesting to the speaker himself the impossibility of such a wound having been self-inflicted by either hand. For another instance: a witness to character, a woman, deposed to the prisoner's being the most amiable of mankind. The figure at that instant stood on the floor before her, looking her full in the face, and pointing out the prisoner's evil countenance with an extended arm and an outstretched finger.

The third change now to be added impressed me strongly as the most marked and striking of all. I do not theorise upon it; I accurately state it, and there leave it. Although the Appearance was not itself perceived by those whom it addressed, its coming close to such persons was invariably attended by some trepidation or disturbance on their part. It seemed to me as if it were prevented, by laws to which I was not amenable, from fully revealing itself to others, and yet as if it could invisibly, dumbly, and darkly overshadow their minds. When the leading counsel for the defence suggested that hypothesis of suicide, and the figure stood at the learned gentleman's elbow, frightfully sawing at its severed throat, it is undeniable that the counsel faltered in his speech, lost for a few seconds the thread of his ingenious discourse, wiped his forehead with his handkerchief, and turned extremely pale. When the witness to character was confronted by the Appearance, her eyes most certainly did follow the direction of its pointed finger, and rest in great hesitation and trouble upon the prisoner's face. Two additional illustrations will suffice. On the eighth day of the trial, after the pause which was every day made early in the afternoon for a few minutes' rest and refreshment, I came back into Court with the rest of the Jury some little time before the return of the Judges. Standing up in the box and looking about me, I thought the figure was not there, until, chancing to raise my eyes to the gallery, I saw it bending forward, and leaning over a very decent woman, as if to assure itself whether the Judges had resumed their seats or not. Immediately afterwards that woman screamed, fainted, and was carried out. So with the venerable, sagacious, and patient Judge who conducted the trial. When the case was over, and he settled himself and his papers to sum up, the murdered man, entering by the Judges' door, advanced to his Lordship's desk, and looked eagerly over his shoulder at the pages of his notes which he was turning. A change came over his Lordship's face; his hand stopped; the peculiar shiver, that I knew so well, passed over him; he faltered, "Excuse me, gentlemen, for a few moments. I am somewhat oppressed by the vitiated air," and did not recover until he had drunk a glass of water.

Through all the monotony of six of those interminable ten days, the same Judges and others on the bench, the same Murderer in the dock, the same lawyers at the table, the same tones of question and answer rising to the roof of the court, the same scratching of the Judge's pen, the same ushers going in and out, the same lights kindled at the same hour when there had been any natural light of day, the same foggy curtain outside the great windows when it was foggy, the same rain pattering and dripping when it was rainy, the same footprints of turnkeys and prisoner day after day on the same sawdust, the same keys locking and unlocking the same heavy doors - through all the wearisome monotony which made me feel as if I had been Foreman of the Jury for a vast period of time, and Piccadilly had flourished coevally with Babylon, the murdered man never lost one trace of his distinctness in my eyes, nor was he at any moment less distinct than anybody else. I must not omit, as a matter of fact, that I never once saw the Appearance which I call by the name of the murdered man look at the Murderer. Again and again I wondered, "Why does he not?" But he never did.

Nor did he look at me, after the production of the miniature, until the last closing minutes of the trial arrived. We retired to consider at seven minutes before ten at night. The idiotic vestryman and his two parochial parasites gave us so much trouble that we twice returned into Court to beg to have certain extracts from the Judge's notes re-read. Nine of us had not the smallest doubt about those passages, neither, I believe, had any one in the Court; the dunder-headed triumvirate, having no idea but obstruction, disputed them for that very reason. At length we prevailed, and finally the Jury returned into Court at ten minutes past twelve.

The murdered man at that time stood directly opposite the Jury-box, on the other side of the Court. As I took my place, his eyes rested on me with great attention; he seemed satisfied, and slowly shook a great gray veil, which he carried on his arm for the first time, over his head and whole form. As I gave in our verdict, "Guilty," the veil collapsed, all was gone, and his place was empty.

The Murderer, being asked by the Judge, according to usage, whether he had anything to say before sentence of Death should be passed upon him, indistinctly muttered something which was described in the leading newspapers of the following day as 'a few rambling, incoherent, and half-audible words, in which he was understood to complain that he had not had a fair trial, because the Foreman of the Jury was prepossessed against him.' The remarkable declaration that he really made was this: "My Lord, I knew I was a doomed man, when the Foreman of my Jury came into the box. My Lord, I knew he would never let me off, because, before I was taken, he somehow got to my bedside in the night, woke me, and put a rope round my neck."

10

When I was ten, I started at a new primary school one day too late to qualify for a place on their Spring break adventure holiday to Dartmoor National Park. Having to stay behind seemed like the end of my world. It wasn't, of course. But for one of the teachers that made the trip to deepest, darkest Devon, it almost certainly was. Early on the fourth day, Mr. ******* set out on a solo hike across the moor and was never seen or heard from again. It's possible he planned his disappearance, and started a new life in a far off exotic location - such as Swanage. But I like to think, particularly after reading Mr. Cole's Cthulhu Mythos classic - set on Bodmin Moor - that he came face to face with an ancient evil and never saw the light of day again. Only joking (I think).

THE HORROR UNDER PENMIRE

by Adrian Cole

Penmire is strewn across the edge of one of the bleakest stretches of Cornish moorland in existence. Though the windswept houses are exposed constantly to the buffets of Atlantic gales, the withdrawn inhabitants live their lives in sheltered seclusion, rarely venturing beyond the proximities of their isolated haven. There are few trees in Penmire, or indeed for miles around on this spectral, misted countryside - the hard outcrops of granite permit only the barest growths of gorse and heather. Any who chance to pass this way would wonder how it is that the villagers live.

Yet, it has been thus for years without number. In its long, unchronicled history, Penmire has tenanted miners, farmers, even smugglers from the secret coves of the not-too-distant coasts, where even today the caves and blow-holes shelter hidden secrets. There have always been people here in Penmire, perhaps from the dawn of man; sometimes it is whispered abroad on shadowed evenings that men worshipped at strange altars in the marshes behind the village, and some folks hold that Arthur took refuge here at one time, pursued across the moors by some hideous foe.

Only the tors of frowning granite know how long Penmire has stood, but the magic of distant ages still hangs wraith-like over the quaint dwellings, suggesting primal antiquity and forgotten knowledge. What scenes of ancient savagery did the imperturbable moon gaze down upon through ragged, storm-rent clouds? What dark arts were practiced, what Neolithic sounds mingled with the roaring winds, to be torn and hurled across miles of barren wasteland?

Now the village seems to slumber, oblivious to the outside world, contemplating, perhaps, its fabled past.

Roy Baxter had long been fascinated by the lure of mystic Penmire. He was a hard-working engineer from Bristol; or "up-country" as the locals termed it, but his hobby was this deep interest in folklore and mythology. It was a hobby which led him all over England, pottering around on ancient sites, and browsing through musty, faded records.

He was on holiday now, driving fairly aimlessly through the enchanting hamlets of Cornwall, the county that perhaps drew him most, and it was here in the tiny pubs that he first heard muted comments about Penmire. It was just the sort of guarded half-secret that he listened out for, but no one was anxious to locate the place for him. His curiosity was fully aroused - he often found the local people non-committal concerning the old legends, despite their talkative natures - for an unnatural barrier of silence would always clamp down the moment he tried to bring Penmire into the conversation. In one little pub, he saw a group of farmers down pints and fairly rush out into the night, though he may have imagined their rapid exit.

Baxter's fertile imagination worked further overtime when he tried to pinpoint Penmire on a map. All his efforts failed. There simply weren't any records of the place anywhere, on Ordnance Survey maps or local records. How could that be possible? It was 1974 for God's sake!

Despite this disappointment, Baxter was thrilled. He was certain the village existed and determined all the more to find it. Acting on the assumption from what little he had heard, that Penmire was somewhere on the central moorlands, he tried to cover as much of that foreboding landscape as he could, but it was a fruitless task. Thick fingers of fog obscured the hidden paths and narrow roadways that could have led him there. Infuriated, he came off the moors and drove into Bodmin, where he checked into a small hotel.

That evening he came down the creaking stairs, ducking under a thick beam, and came into the foyer.

"May I use the phone?" he asked his dumpy, rosy-cheeked hostess. She was a cheerful soul, ample-bosomed and bouncy, typical of the loquacious landladies he was familiar with.

"'Course you can, Mr. Baxter," she chirped in a high voiced, elongating her 'r's' in the uniquely Cornish fashion.

"Fine. I want to call London, actually."

"Oh, that's all right. Business, I s'pose?" Mrs. Harcott was all smiles. She was already imagining Baxter to be a big-time executive or possibly a TV producer. Her gossip circles would shortly be afire with the news.

"Yes," Baxter grinned, thinking it would all go on the bill anyway. "Oh, by the way," he added, trying to sound casual, "I noticed a turning on the moor for a place called - what was it?

- ah, Penmire. Yes, that was it, Penmire. It seems I've heard of it in local customs and the like. Only I'm rather keen on that sort of thing. Do you know the place at all?" He had lied about that turn-off, but he wanted to see if Mrs. Harcott would deny all knowledge of Penmire. Her mouth was slightly open, as though he had taken her by surprise. She began idly flicking through her guest-book, and Baxter knew he had found another peculiar link in the mysterious armour of that moorland village.

"Well, I 'ave 'eard of it, Mr. Baxter, but I can't say as I know where 'tis. I 'spect you'd find out in the bar tonight, though. We do 'ave some of the local landlords in 'ere sometimes. But I'd keep away if I were you, Mr Baxter. 'Tis awful bleak up there, 'specially with the mist."

"I see. Well, thanks anyway, Mrs. Harcott. Perhaps you're right." That was all he'd get out of her. So the place did exist.

"You're welcome," she returned, but her air of pleasantness had dissipated. Baxter found the phone tucked away in a convenient niche, and after a series of brief interchanges eventually got through to a London number.

"Hello, Phil? This is Roy."

There was a pause before he heard the voice of his life-long friend. "Hello, there! Long time no see. What have you been doing with yourself? Are you at home?" Philip Dayton's voice was warm, firm, painting a picture of a strong character.

"No, I'm in Cornwall, actually."

"Ah, the legend-haunted South West," Dayton chuckled. He was more than familiar with his friend's obsession with mythology. Himself an expert in the field, he guessed the reason for this call at once. Roy was 'on to something.' Dayton grinned to himself as he thought of some of the ridiculous 'finds' his pal had unearthed in the last few years.

"Yes," said Baxter. "I've got a few weeks off to pursue my true calling as usual."

"Very nice. And what have you dug up from the pixie-infested tin mines this time?"

"Well, nothing as yet. But I've come across an interesting case."

"Oh?" Dayton was intrigued by his friend's tone, for, despite Baxter's ability to stumble across events of absolutely no importance whatsoever, he did occasionally find something interesting.

"Ever heard of Penmire?"

"Penmire? No, can't place it offhand."

"It's a small village on Bodmin Moor, but I don't know where. If you can't direct me to it, no one can." Baxter sounded urgent. He knew Philip Dayton's knowledge of legend and folklore was extensive; Dayton had written several authoritative books on the subject, and had read as much material as he could find.

"Ah, Penmire. It does ring the faintest of bells. Vaguely connected with Arthur, and with a history of Druidic dabblings to boot. Yes, I know of it, though I can't tell you the gory details until I've dredged them up."

"Well, it's a start," exclaimed Baxter. "Where the blue blazes is the place?"

"That I don't know. In fact I think you're in a blind alley, old sport. As far as I remember the place is only legendary anyway. A bit like the evasive Camelot."

"Oh no!" Baxter groaned. "Don't tell me it doesn't exist!"

"I'm not sure. I'm not too well up in those channels. Tell you what, though."

"Uh-huh?"

"Where are you, exactly?"

Baxter gave his address and his friend took it down.

"Bodmin, eh? You hang on down there, and perhaps have a scout round for our hidden Penmire. In the meantime, I'll see what I can find out about it at this end, then I might just drive down and join you."

"You needn't do that, Phil, thanks all the same. I don't want to drag you off on a wild goose chase."

There was a laugh from the other end of the line. "Nonsense. I'm hooked. Matter of fact I'm at a loose end at the moment. I've just finished a series of university lectures, and I had thought about going up to the Yorkshire Moors for a spot of research. Witches and all that. But I must admit, Bodmin Moor sounds just as enterprising."

"Working on a new book?"

"Yup. Haven't done a damn thing yet, though. So your little find might furnish me with a few new titbits. I could do with a break, and I haven't drunk a few jars with you for far too long."

"Great. In that case I'll stick around. When will you be here?"

"Oh, say three days. I should be able to ferret something out by then."

"Right. Give my love to Annie and the kids." Baxter rang off.

Philip Dayton scratched his head irritably and sipped his scotch, his thoughts running back once more to the events of the last few days. Where the hell was Roy? Five days ago he'd phoned him, enthusing about Penmire and its superstitious connotations. Two days ago, he, Dayton, had arrived here in Bodmin with enough information to help find the place, but Roy was nowhere to be found. That just wasn't like him.

Dayton now sat in the cramped bar of his friend's hotel, where he, too, had checked in. No one had been able to help. Mrs. Harcott had seen Roy leave shortly after phoning him, and his few things were still in his room. She hadn't seen him since. Dayton had made several abortive attempts to eke information out of the people who used the bar, but he got the same shrugs from all of them. Hardly anyone had seen him, anyway, as he'd left the hotel shortly after checking in.

Dayton got little sleep that night: he began to get progressively more worried. His eyes turned again and again to the monolith on the hill above Bodmin, which stood out clearly against the purple skies. He turned this way and that in a restless half-slumber, while the brass pixies on the mantelpiece seemed to contort themselves into weird shapes. In the early hours of the morning, Dayton settled on a plan of action: he couldn't hang around lamely any longer. Roy must have found Penmire, otherwise he would have been back.

After a hurried breakfast, Dayton drove up on to Bodmin Moor and began searching the headless side-roads and lesser tracks, from time to time consulting a rough map he had improvised in the records section of a London library. He pulled up at the base of a chain of huge, jutting tors, crowned with bare outcrops of wind-swept rock. According to his information, Penmire should be on the other side. There was an old road somewhere, but the chances were that it would be overgrown and hard to find.

Dayton got out, locking the car, and began the steep climb, his feet sinking slightly into the moss that dotted these lower slopes. It was a gorgeous day; for once the sky was free of clouds and the sun beat down, giving the usual foreboding landscape a more welcoming quality. It was July; typically hot and airless. He could hear the skylarks twittering incessantly, though they were too high up to be seen against the glare. As he climbed he felt fresh and alive; at one with the land. His doubts about Roy dispersed in the joy of the climb.

As he reached the rock sentinels on top of the tor, Dayton let out a deep sigh, mopped his brow and looked back at the clear vista below him. Far off he saw the sun glinting on the metal of speeding cars as they raced down the main road. You're missing it all, he thought. After a moment he turned and clambered through the dark rocks which were splotched her and there with thin patches of lichen. Once he'd crossed the top of the tor, he looked down with a satisfied grunt at the straggling houses below.

Unless I miss my guess, that'll be Penmire - picturesque little spot, he mused. A sparkling stream ran out of the distant village, twisting its way into the limits of his vision, where a dark mass of trees formed a wood at the edge of the moors. Before Penmire lay the marshes, a flattish area, peppered with bogs and mires, which the old records had mentioned, and behind them rose another series of rugged tors, leading off hazily into the heart of the moorland.

Dayton was about to start the descent, when he heard muffled voices somewhere behind him. At least, he thought they had come from behind him. He turned, half expecting to see a basking courting couple, but his gaze encountered only the blank rocks. Damn fool, he said to himself. On a day like this, voices carried a long way.

He took off his jacket, slung it unceremoniously over his shoulder and began to climb down into the broad valley. He hadn't noticed it, but the skylarks were no longer audible. Looking down on Penmire, he could see it was oddly lifeless, as though it had been long abandoned. That was strange, because according to Dayton's information it should be populated. Still, he was some way off yet, though he couldn't see any vehicles or telephone wires. To all intents and purposes the place was dead.

As he pressed on, expecting to see at least a sheep or two, Dayton was suddenly aware of the silence, broken only by his passage through the tufts of reed. He stood still and realised just how absurdly quiet it was. He was reminded of Alice stepping through the looking-glass. So where is the white rabbit? He felt eyes on him, too, though he had to suppress a chuckle at his own nerves. Perhaps the villagers had seen him approach - in a place as remote as this they wouldn't appreciate strangers. He should have been able to hear the birds or at least the teeming insect life: the grasshoppers and crickets usually made a terrific din.

Behind him, towering up into the sunlight, the rocks seemed to leer down, mockingly. Dayton shrugged and moved on. Roy's car should be around somewhere, he told himself. He'd feel a lot easier when he saw it. He heard the faintest suggestion of voices again and cursed himself; he put it down to exertion - after all, he was not a young man. Penmire was still some way off when he noticed a sudden chill in the air. The psychical research boys would love this place. Then he laughed inwardly as he saw the reason for the drop in temperature.

Coming across the brow of a nearby tor was a thick mist, lapping over the rocks and over-spilling into the valley. These moor mists can be frightening to those who don't know them. They appear from almost nowhere and literally descend like blankets in a matter of minutes. Dayton had tramped Dartmoor to the east, and knew how quickly he would be enveloped by those swirling, silent tendrils.

He speeded up his descent, certain now he could hear those indefinable voices. It was uncanny, made even more so by this thickening mist. The stuff seemed to tremble with animation as it reached out and engulfed him. Dayton calculated that he had about a mile to go. He stumbled on, muttering obscenities, through the gathering coils.

There then burst on his ears a chorus of sounds that stopped him dead in his tracks. He was in the heart of the mist when, as if at a given signal, thousands of frogs burst into voice, the sound of their deep croaking coming from all around the valley. Dayton reflected that it was the most chilling sound he had ever heard. He tried to see into the mist, but out of all those countless frogs he could see none. He was scared, no use in pretending otherwise, but he smiled grimly. The mist had probably alarmed them. Sitting at home in an armchair was one thing, but when you were alone in this lot it was a different matter.

Far off he heard a splashing vaguely over the cacophony of frogs. That would be the stream, etching its way through the boulders. But this was too rhythmic for a stream, more as though someone were sloshing their way through water or mud. An inhabitant at last? Dayton thought of shouting, but the sound appeared to recede, and, for some unaccountable reason, he thought it had gone underground. So many odd things had occurred already that he cursed himself and carried on.

Abruptly the frogs were silent, and an abysmal silence supplanted their terrible racket. Dayton scraped his shins more than once, now only vaguely certain of the direction in which Penmire lay. His progress had become far more difficult, as he had to skirt sinking clods of peat and slime-covered pools of mire. He was sweating profusely, his face damp with mist. Where was that blasted village? He rested against a huge granite slab and wheezed. Roy, my son, heads shall roll for this.

The events of the next few seconds were a total shock to him, and concrete proof that something was very much amiss with this weird valley. The rock on which he was leaning seemed to twitch, as the flank of a horse twitches when irritated by a fly. Dayton drew back in horrified alarm, half expecting something dark and malign to rear up out of the mire. Then the earth heaved, and he pitched forward into the soaking reeds. "This is ridiculous!" he kept saying, over and over again, but the ground rippled as though it was water, and Dayton bit off a scream.

It must be an island of turf, he told himself desperately, for anything else would be far too alien to accept. He struggled to his feet and ran, though it was like standing in a small boat. He stumbled again before the movements stopped, then rushed on as far as the reeds and hidden rocks would allow. This time he could definitely hear voices, though they seemed as much inside him as out in those sentient mists. The voices laughed, chuckling insanely at his plight: voices which he knew instinctively were not human.

The mist was now as thick as the fogs he knew in London. God, how far away all that was. On and on he wandered, his shins bruised and bleeding from innumerable bumps on the hard granite that lay obscured everywhere he turned. A rumbling like distant thunder caught his attention, coming from the marsh, and again it seemed to emanate from under the earth. Yet that was unthinkable.

Dayton's progress had slowed right down, his breath coming in laboured gasps. The mist was playing tricks, though the sound had receded. Now all he could hear was the drip, drip of moisture on the leaves, faint though that sound was. Something dark and suggestive loomed up ahead, and he fell to his knees, heart pounding like a locomotive. God, this is it!

But it was only a house. He had reached the sanctuary of Penmire at last.

Painfully he limped between two houses, their eaves overhanging the path, their windows dark and shadowed. As he came into the street, he still had no idea where to start looking for Roy, assuming he was here. It was a relief to get off the marsh. Something stirred in the mist, and he recoiled in surprise. The skulking shape of a cat slunk past, eyes blazing with green hate, eyes that never left his own.

Where is everyone? Still the dense mist showed no sign of lifting. Dayton stumbled on up the badly kept street, hands thrust deep in his pockets, numb with the cold, jacket pulled tight around him. He was conscious now of other cat-like shapes padding around the edge of his vision, but they were always obscured by the mist. At last he saw a dim light, and, coming upon what appeared to be an old inn, he pushed the thick wooden door and went inside.

Hostile eyes regarded him as he closed the door. A bar ran the length of the far wall, while several tables were placed here and there around the little room. The walls were fitted with panelled cubicles, and nailed to the roofbeams were brass horse accoutrements, though Dayton couldn't see any horseshoes. He wasn't surprised.

An old woman sat at one of the tables, arms resting on a gnarled stick, a battered bag on the floor beside her slippered feet. Two weather-beaten men sat in one of the chipped cubicles in the corner, smoking and playing cards. The barman, a huge, shirt-sleeved character with a pink, freckled face and thinning, sandy hair, was talking to what appeared to be a local labourer. There was thick mud on his boots. The barman scowled at Dayton as he came forward.

"We aren't open yet," he said gruffly in a very strong accent. Dayton noticed a grubby collie lying at the labourer's feet, regarding him disdainfully.

"That's all right. Only I, uh, lost my way in this ruddy mist. It's a bit marshy out there and I don't fancy trying to find my way back to the car until the mist lifts."

The old lady regarded him through her spectacles, but never blinked. She might have been carved from granite for all she moved. No one spoke. Dayton edged nearer the bar, wary of the dog. Its owner had turned to inspect him, his gaze as scathing as his animal's. The card players had stopped.

"I don't suppose you've a phone..."

"No. There ain't none in Penmire," returned the barman, taking a rag and wiping down the bar slowly and methodically.

"Oh. Well, I'm in a bit of a mess. Is there anywhere I can clean up?"

The eyes stared questioningly. Christ, thought Dayton, what are they - zombies?

"I'm, er, looking for a friend of mine. I believe he's staying in Penmire."

The woman nodded and looked at him vaguely. "Thought 'e was from outside."

"Hush, Mrs. Dinnock," muttered the barman. "I think you're mistaken, sir."

"Oh, but my friend expressly stated he would be here." Dayton watched the thick pipe smoke curling up into the beams from the corner.

"No, I don't think so. No one has come. Only you."

Dayton shifted his gaze to the card players. They sat as though paralysed. What if Roy hadn't come here? "Perhaps he'll turn up later. In the meantime, have you a gents handy? I must try and clean up a bit."

"Through there," grunted the barman reluctantly, pointing to a side door.

Dayton nodded his thanks and went through. He found a tiny toilet and closed the flaking door behind him. There was an overpowering smell of fish exuding from the drain. Now what? he asked himself as he washed his hands in the battered sink. I was better off in the ruddy marsh.

He returned to the bar to find it empty, save for the inhospitable barman, who tried his damnedest to ignore him.

"You get this mist often?"

"Ah."

Dayton decided it was an affirmative. "Like pea soup, eh?" he said, grinning, but it had no effect. Now I know how the lepers used to feel, he mused. "Any chance of me buying a bite to eat?"

"Don't serve meals, sir. There's a shop down the street."

"I'll hang on here till the mist lifts, I think. You, er, don't mind?" You hadn't better, he added to himself.

"May be down for a week. Often stops longer in the warm weather. My advice is to take the road off the moor, sir. You'll be all right. Folks in Penmire is wary of strangers." The barman was fiddling about with glasses and glimpsing at a paper, anything to avoid being drawn into a conversation.

"So I noticed. You, uh, sure about that friend of mine?"

"Positive."

"Okay." Dayton went over to one of the booths and sat down, pretending to study a map he carried. The barman eyed him coldly and began cleaning glasses again. Outside, everything remained silent.

Dayton had been seated for only a short time when he noticed a book of some description poking up from the back of the seat opposite. Gently he reached over, careful not to be seen by the barman who had for a moment turned to his shelves, and picked it up. It was a paperback entitled, *Myths and Folklore of the South West*.

That clinched it! It must be Roy's. Hastily Dayton flicked through the book and found several underlined passages and notations, all in pencil and instantly recognisable as Roy's handwriting. He found a section on Druidic practices and certain other primitive rights said to have been handed down from earlier periods. The name Arthur cropped up here and there, along with the usual references to Tintagel. Then Dayton found a very brief passage on Penmire.

"... a very old settlement, believed to be the one-time centre of a very primitive culture, centred around the worship of the sea... fantastic theory that the earliest inhabitants were settlers from the sinking of Atlantis... seems a rather fanciful notion... possibly the survivors from Lyonesse or counterpart..." Pencilled beside the passage was the word: DAGON?

"I'm closing now," boomed a voice above Dayton. He slammed the book shut with a start.

"Oh. Oh, really? I'll be off then. Always carry some light reading matter, you know." He knows, Dayton thought. What are these people hiding? He forced a grin, reflecting that it was still relatively early.

"Keep on the road, sir. One step off and you're likely to sink for good in the marshes."

Dayton rose, pocketing the book. "Uh-huh. I expect it'll brighten up soon. Sorry to be a nuisance." He left as casually as he could, stepping once more into the dank, oppressive mist. The stench of fish came even more strongly to his nostrils now. Still, he'd resigned himself to expect anything in this eerie place; even pixies. But he was being observed, he knew at once, and far more intensely than before. Then he saw the glowing, baleful eyes of the cats, never for a moment averting their gaze.

Dayton watched them as he started down the street, having decided to stop at the shop. To his horror, he saw there were now a number of dogs in the mist, all plodding along quietly, as though waiting for the command to attack. This was fast becoming a nightmare. What had Roy meant by the pencilled 'Dagon?' Dayton recognised the name as that of a mythical sea-dwelling creature, though as far as he knew it had only appeared in fiction.

Faintly defined houses slipped past as he hastily moved on, conscious now of several cats and dogs lurking at his heels like a hungry pack. A flapping from above made him duck, to see a crow disappear into the gloom. Another house appeared ahead, but before he had taken another step he saw three pairs of eyes glowing in front of him.

What are they - wolves? He felt panic gripping him. They're trying to surround me! He abruptly turned to his left and sprinted between the houses, anywhere to escape the lurking shadows. A bark behind him told him they were giving chase.

He came to the edge of the marsh, and for a moment he almost forgot the pursuit. He had found concrete proof that Roy had come to Penmire: one wheel and part of the front bumper of his Rover 2000 were sticking up out of the mire. Dayton had no time to speculate. Something heavy crashed into the back of his head and he plummeted into a bottomless well of oblivion.

Dayton came round with a splitting headache. His arms felt as though they were being torn from their sockets, and his mouth was horribly dry. Total darkness enveloped him; his surroundings swam in a blur as he tried to focus on something tangible. Vague thoughts on what had happened trickled back to him, but he was in no condition to struggle.

The first sound he heard was the plop-plop-plop of water somewhere near his head. He tried to move, only to find he was chained up, back to a damp wall, somewhere in a cellar or cave. Chained? His mind raced as he tugged hopelessly in the chill, earthy air. There were scurrying sounds around his feet in response to his movements; he kicked out wildly, his toe digging into a number of squealing, furry bodies. The place was alive with rats, and as they ran hither and thither; the air became permeated with the now familiar stink of rotting fish.

"Phil!" hissed a voice nearby, where more chains rattled in the acrid blackness.

"Roy? Is that you?" Dayton could not believe his ears.

"'Fraid so, old pal. I was hoping you wouldn't get to find me."

"What the devil's going on in this village? I've never encountered anything like it in all my travels."

"I dread to think." Baxter sounded very tired.

"The rudeness of the local goons I can stomach, but this is going too damn far."

"Guess so. But save your strength, Phil. You'll probably need it."

"I found a book of yours in the inn. I notice you've pencilled in a few notes. Have you any idea what's happening? Why the chains, for God's sake?" Rivulets of sweat trickled down Dayton's face, despite the cold. His arms ached intolerably.

"Something very old and very evil has got Penmire in its grip, Phil. Whether they practice satanic rites or what, I don't know, but I've been shackled up here for bloody ages. I don't know for how long. I can't feel my arms. Some of the things I've heard - God, it's incredible!"

"Where exactly are we?"

"Under the chapel. You may have noticed it. Sort of crypt. Judging by some of the chanting that goes on up there."

"What have you done for food? You must have been here for several days."

"Oh, they keep me alive. Christ knows why, but they feed me. A robed figure in black appears now and again. It would be laughably melodramatic if it wasn't for the fact that I'm scared. Really scared, Phil. We're in a helluva situation."

Dayton admired his friend's strength of character; a lesser man would have cracked up in here. Even he might...

It's insane," he growled. "I know about witchcraft and most of its various cults, but I can't believe these people would do us any serious harm. It must be some sort of hoax - a festival, do you think?" Dayton's nerves were rapidly fraying. He had to keep talking.

"The pain's real enough."

"They'd never get away with it."

"Oh, no? What's to say the police will find us in the mire? It's endless. No one is safe on these moors. It's one of the bleakest parts of England. We may as well be on Mars."

"Cheerful bugger!" They were silent for a moment; the humour soon vanished.

"Well," grunted Dayton at length, "what do we do?"

"God knows. We can't break these chains. We just wait."

So they waited, their minds uselessly trying to fathom a way to escape, but there was absolutely none. The seconds slipped into minutes, marked by the ever-dripping, wet walls, and the minutes turned slowly into hours. There was only the pain and discomfort as the scampering rats kept vigil over the two incarcerated men. At last they heard sounds above them - feet shuffling to and fro in the chapel. Dayton, who had slipped to his knees, cocked an ear. Faintly came the strain of weird, ethereal music, like fluted pipes, drifting out from the old walls into the night.

"Roy. Are you awake?" There was a grunt. "What's that noise?"

"It's them again. It happens every now and then - nights, I suppose... Another... ritual."

"You okay?"

"I'll do. You know that passage I marked in the book? Did you see my reference to Dagon?"

"Yes. The book's in my pocket."

"Well, there could be something in it. It's a crazy notion, but now and then I've heard the name Dagon mentioned in the chanting. You listen for it, once they start. One time I thought I heard something... out in the marsh. Like a huge wave breaking. Yes, I know it sounds bloody daft, but there was something."

"Maybe not so daft, Roy. I came here across the marsh and some of the things I heard were pretty odd."

"Such as?"

"People splashing about. And frogs. God, I never heard so many. All at once they started up in unison."

They fell silent again. Baxter broke the lull with a forced snort. "Humph! We're probably behaving like kids. I know we're in a right mess, but the moor is spooky. There are probably the usual scientific explanations for it all."

"Perhaps. But I'd like a good explanation for this." Dayton rattled his chains. "I'll create bloody hell when I get back to civilisation."

"Quiet a sec!" They both listened anew to the strange noises from above. A deep, somehow obscene chanting had begun, the words totally indecipherable, utterly alien.

"There they go again. They'll go on for hours, working themselves up into a frenzy. Just when you think it'll die down, they start up again."

"This is all new to me. I wish I had a tape-recorder."

"I'd settle for a wrench," Baxter replied, but neither of them laughed.

All that night the blasphemous sound swelled until, in the early hours of the morning, it reached a peak. There were sounds from around the prisoners, sounds of slopping footsteps, though nothing could be seen in the dark; the fish odour was overpowering. The climax of the terrible dirge above came in a resounding thunderclap which shook the very foundations of the chapel. Its echoes rolled away into the distance.

"Roy, that sound! It's going away beneath us. I'm sure of it."

"Eh?" Baxter was exhausted, very drowsy, having only partly registered the boom. He couldn't take much more of this.

"Have you heard anything underground?" persisted Dayton.

"Underground? No. Only from up there," Baxter said sleepily.

Dayton was thinking of the marsh and the rippling motion

that he had seen.

"Probably an echo," Baxter suggested. "There are lots of caves under the village."

"Caves?"

"Well, tunnels. I saw a few of them when they dragged me in here. All man-made, though."

"So what about the mire?" Caves running under that would be geologically impossible.

"I dunno. They seem to avoid that." Baxter yawned.

"Curious." The two men lapsed into fitful sleep; time had ceased to exist for them in this rancid pit.

They languished for three days; three days of gruelling anguish which were broken only by the brief appearance of a robed, half-glimpsed figure who fed them. After that, the villagers came for their prisoners. Above the cellar, the voices had begun chanting again in mournful unison. From out of the ether came whispered sounds of demonic laughter. Baxter and Dayton were too spent to complain as their chains were unlocked, and they were forced, staggering, through numerous cold puddles of muddy water, pushed along by the sinister robed figures of a score of unseen inhabitants.

They were led almost unconsciously along these subterranean, winding tunnels until they came out eventually into the open. Their bodies were weak and their spirits broken.

It was evening as they emerged; the sun was sinking into an orange sea of clouds, tinting the surrounding tors with gold. Wisps of glistening mist hung in shreds above the marsh, like steam rising from a sulphurous pool. The two men registered little of this. They were some distance from the village, at the edge of the marsh, and here they were thrust forward on to a huge, flat slab of granite. Thin beards of stubble darkened both their jaws, while their eyes were rimmed and bloodshot. Neither had the strength to look up at the diminishing glory of the sunset.

Roy Baxter began to mutter to himself, reciting the Lord's Prayer under his breath. Dayton's head lay against cold rock. He regarded his friend through pain-misted eyes; beside him the reeds trembled in the cool breeze.

"Roy. Roy!" he whispered hoarsely. The other turned to him, still praying. Above them the captors were still.

"We're done. Do you understand?"

"Listen!"

Far out over the marsh there came a gibbering of something nebulous, as though the mire itself were alive. The frogs had begun again that heart-stopping croaking - a hundred thousand throats swelling the chorus. Dayton turned his head, forcing a look back at the village, framed between the arms of two of the gaunt figures in black. There were scores of similarly garbed people filing out of what he took to be the chapel, all with arms raised in supplication, all walking like jerky dolls toward the two outsiders and the marsh.

To whom or what are they praying? Dayton asked himself, unable to credit his eyes. With a start of revulsion he saw there were a number of dogs, cats and even a few sheep staring placidly out at the marsh. The spell on Penmire gripped even the animals. The chant swelled and the words became clear, though still incomprehensible.

"Ngah ohahgn, mnah, ohahgn mnepn phatagn Dagon.

Ngah opahgan, rhantgna Dagon.

Ssna, ssna, phatagn Dagon."

Over and over they repeated it. These words were not written for human mouths to speak. I must get out now - God knows what they'll do, thought Dayton.

"Roy!" he whispered. "Roy!" But his friend had passed out over the altar-like stone. Dayton feigned the same, one eye on the chanting crowd. Those around had taken up the chant as well. Bloody mumbo-jumbo.

All around the valley the sound of the frogs was growing in volume; louder and louder it came, blending malefic ally with the ululations of the oncoming worshippers. From the marshes came a rising cloud of dense vapour, and with it the unbearable fish stench that Dayton had smelled so frequently. This time it seemed to pulse out from the marsh in disgusting waves, and he almost vomited.

Now he could see the frogs. They hopped around the stone as if mocking him - the marshes were teeming with them. Dayton shook himself. Beside him his captors were kneeling, arms outstretched in obeisance to the very heart of the marsh. What did they expect to see? Dayton craned his neck and gasped. Bubbles were bursting all over the surface as if it were boiling. He fought to control his sanity as he realised the chanting was attracting something out in that festering pool of horror.

A movement beside him drew his attention back to his immediate dilemma. He turned to see some of these devilish acolytes stretching Roy, still unconscious, over the altar stone, preparing him for the very sacrifice he had feared. Dayton was stunned. Not today. Not in this age. Yet they paid no attention to his torrent of invective. Dayton flung himself upon them with last reserves of energy, kicking, biting, hammering with his fists. It was useless. He was flung contemptuously aside to roll pathetically into the reeds.

Stark terror gripped him now. He got up, his movement ignored by the still chanting villagers, and fled into the treacherous mire, desperately trying to find a way through the numerous bogs. He looked back as he panted on, only to see a curved knife, glittering in the twilight with scarlet jewels, raised high. This is madness, madness. Dayton averted his gaze and felt his stomach heave, refusing to believe the knife would fall. Yet he heard it sink into Roy Baxter's flesh, and a shuddering, satisfied sigh went up from the villagers.

"Abaghna pnam pnam Dagon.

Accept our sacrifice, O Dagon.

Ssna, ssna, phatagn Dagon."

Tears of disbelief coursed in grimy runnels down Dayton's face. He shook his head in utter disgust at what they had done. Blood ran freely over the altar into the mud – Roy had died without a sound. Dayton fled further into the marsh, hoping against hope to reach the tors before the mob came for him. However, further diabolic events were unfolding. From even the farthest reaches of the marsh, the fish smell was at its most foul; a new element of horror was emerging.

Unspeakable shapes were thrusting up out of the oozing mud and green scum, shapes so dreadful, so appalling, that only in the wildest fantasies of a madman could they have been conceived. Dayton bit into his hand to stifle a shriek. The constant chanting was taking its toll, as had the spilling of blood, drawing these vile monstrosities up from the depths like enchanted snakes. They were half human, half fish, or so it looked, for their features were a peculiar blend of both, with fins protruding from each jowl and long, plumed spines stretching right down their backs. There were gills in their man-like trunks, and their eyes were the wide, filmy eyes of fish; their arms long and thin, tapering to webbed claws.

From these creatures came the hellish smell. Dayton reached

a boulder and leapt on to it, his heart almost bursting with the effort. The mist was thickening, thankfully obscuring many of the beings, while the sun had set, leaving the world in rapidly gathering darkness. Dayton was surrounded by the fishmen, who still continued to rise from the muck like a legion from Hell itself. As he stared in fascination, they began emitting croaking sounds of their own, frog-like and deep, until with a shudder Dayton realised they were chanting in response to the people of Penmire.

From thick, fleshy lips came the same dread words the villagers were chanting, spoken, he saw, by the very ones to whom the language belonged. Although he was some way out in the marsh, none of the terrible people came near. They just waved and writhed gently from side to side as though drugged, arms raised in ecstasy as were those of the villagers. Frogs jumped everywhere, their croaks adding to the swelling din.

Dayton ached with weariness; there was not a muscle in his body that didn't crave rest, but he knew that he must keep on while the horde was preoccupied with its incantations. He sprang from the rock and zigzagged his faltering way through islands of turf, constantly sinking to his knees into clinging mud. He wanted to lie down and sleep, but dare not. The thought of that dripping knife gave him more will to go on. Still the creatures were ignoring him, though he passed within feet of several, shutting everything out of his mind except the tors and escape.

Suddenly, the ground heaved, pitching him forward into the gurgling slime, so that for terrifying seconds he crawled with cold, reptilian frogs. Within moments he was knee-deep in them, jerking himself upright and yanking his arms to try to free them. They came out of the mud with great sucking sounds, but his feet were held. He beat frantically at the swarming frogs, feeling them squirming beneath him in multitudes. He struggled in despair. He was trapped. And still the chanting went on, rising in volume, driving him ever closer to madness. Now the ground began rippling and pulsing like a great heart beating. A note of joy had entered the chanting.

Dayton heard, felt, the sound from below. He could not put a name to it, nor dare do so. Excitement spurred the invocations around him, and he tried to twist and see what exactly the villagers were doing: were they pursuing, or had they forgotten him in the midst of their insane revels? He could not see. He was stuck firmly, sinking inexorably to a gruesome death.

"Ngah ohahgn, phatagn Dagon.

Abaghna pnam pnam hnam Dagon.

Accept our second sacrifice, O Dagon.

Ssna, ssna, phatagn Dagon."

Dayton heard the words of the people behind, and the terrible implication. He had escaped the knife, but the mire would take him. Unless... With a last, vain effort, he stripped off his jacket, ready to throw it in front of him in one final attempt to heave himself out. Then he stopped, eyes wide in utter disbelief. Before him the marsh was heaving and thrashing like the cauldron of a volcano, sending great plumes of mud high into the mist. Dayton felt more tremors in the rumbling ground.

The chanting had abruptly ceased, together with the croaking of the frogs, as all eyes, all arms, had turned to the source of the disturbance. From out of the unknown depths of the mire, ringed by the evil-smelling fish creatures, something huge, something unutterably ancient was rising. Dayton screamed now, his whole body shaking uncontrollably, unable to free itself from the fatal clutches of the marsh.

Higher and higher rose the mire-coated colossus, and the unholy stench of that awesome thing grew worse. For this was Dagon, Dagon the ageless, summoned at last from an eternal sleep, summoned from the refuge he had sought untold aeons before, when he and all his kind were cursed upon the earth.

Up, up rose the towering horror, a throbbing, glistening mass of scaly, amorphous life. Waves of mud, spilling over with frogs, rippled out from the growing monster. A score of thick, oily, tentacle-like protuberances, coated in contracting suckers, whipped up from beneath the ooze in a welter of steaming filth, as the titanic creature rose higher, exuding an aura of clinging vapours. Dayton coughed as he caught the first whiffs of the poisonous diffusion; he had sunk waist deep before the thing, his eyes riveted on this being from before the dawn of men.

All around in the night, the servants bowed down, eager in their devotions, smiting themselves and yelling out in exultation. Dagon of the deeps had come. Come to begin a new reign. The earth shook constantly, hissing with escaping steam, and the mire over spilled its contaminated ooze out into the village. Dayton closed his eyes and preyed fervently, sinking lower, lower. Dagon stretched out his many arms to receive the sacrifice his people had prepared.

I see your candle is burning low.

Not to worry, you can always light another.

Oh... You don't have another.

Blow it out to preserve what little light you have left.

You might need it ...

before sunrise ...

to investigate a noise ...

close to you ...

In the dark.

Good night.

Printed in Poland
by Amazon Fulfillment
Poland Sp. z o.o., Wrocław